Dual
Issues

Dual Issues

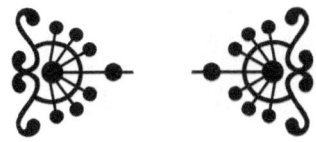

Ria Bonneamie

REGENT PRESS
Berkeley, California

[Paperback]
ISBN 10: 1-58790-717-8
ISBN 13: 978-1-58790-717-3

[E-Book]
ISBN 10: 1-58790-718-6
ISBN 13: 978-1-58790-718-0

Library of Congress Control Number:2025917005

The persons and events in this book are fictional. Names and places have no relevance to any real facts. Any coincidence should be examined thoroughly for cosmic consequences. Canines and other domesticated creatures must be respected, for initially they are innocent, until transformed by humans.

Manufactured in the U.S.A.
REGENT PRESS
Berkeley, California
www.regentpress.net

For Colby, an angel on earth,

And for all my southwestern friends,
You'll recognize some of the places,
but you're not in there, only the bears are real.

HERMAPHRODITUS:

"In Greek mythology, Hermaphroditus was a being partly male, partly female. A legend of the Hellenistic period made Hermaphroditus a beautiful youth, the son of Hermes and Aphrodite. A nymph near a fountain he was bathing in became enamored of him and entreated the gods that she might be forever united with him. The result was the formation of a being half man, half woman."

— ENCYCLOPEDIA BRITANNICA

ANDROGYNY:

We are all androgynous, having experienced lifetimes as both men and women.

— WINAFRED BLAKE LUCAS

TWO SPIRIT PEOPLE:

"Nádleehí [or Náhleeh] is the name for 'Two Spirit People' in the Navajo culture, feminine men born biologically male but functioning socially as women. [Dilbaa is the name for Two Spirit masculine women.] Two Spirit people are seen as having a biological sex that does not match their spirit gender. They are linked to their ancestral spirits. They are regarded as having special sensory qualities. They exist to honor all living things as sacred."

— NAVAJO SCHOLAR WESLEY THOMAS

Table of Contents

Chapter 1 .... First Bear / 11

Chapter 2 .... Birds and Lions / 23

Chapter 3 .... The Walking Four Ranch / 35

Chapter 4 .... Juggling Cases / 45

Chapter 5 .... A Gifted Angel / 52

Chapter 6 .... Yet Another Case / 65

Chapter 7 .... Rosetta Stones / 71

Chapter 8 .... Friends or Foes / 78

Chapter 9 .... Many Ghosts / 85

Chapter 10 .... Joy Ride / 94

Chapter 11 .... A Black Dog / 102

Chapter 12 .... Three Bears / 107

Chapter 13 .... Bad Boys / 114

Chapter 14 .... The Bait / 120

Chapter 15 .... Tying Up Loose Ends / 124

Chapter 16 .... The Trap / 129

Chapter 17 .... A Rustling Party / 134

Chapter 18 .... The Bears' Meeting / 139

Chapter 19 .... Revelry / 142

Chapter One

First Bear

THE WINDING ROAD CLIMBED ON ONE SIDE OF A narrow bubbling creek, twisted past steep salmon-colored cliffs, then unfurled into a steady grid of Ponderosa pines. Right after a sharp curve, the twins surprised a young bear standing on its rear legs, harvesting green, low-hanging acorns from a large oak tree. It turned its head around to stare at them for a few seconds, clearly annoyed by the intrusion, before lowering itself on all fours. In the back seat of their pick-up truck, Tillie, the twins' one-year-old puppy softly growled. The bear took another look at the halted car, slowly shook its head a couple of times, its shiny dark brown coat twinkling in the dappled light, before ambling out of sight into the shaded creek bed.

As they topped the high pass of the Black Range, in southwest New Mexico, the vista of a drier land opened up in front of them. In the distance, dark, smoky-blue mountains framed the horizon line. Blue jays and ravens patrolled the roads overhead. A few miles past a sleepy village, jagged peaks, spires and rounded boulders in various shades of buff, rose again on both sides of the road, amongst a background of mostly pinyon and juniper trees.

After following the barely flowing Percha Creek, they stopped for a plate of spicy enchiladas at La Manzanita, a small restaurant in Hillsboro, a quiet little town trying hard to survive, out of the way from the main trails. While waiting for their order, staring outside the window at the occasional vehicles passing by, they reflected on the first new client they had visited that Monday morning.

~ ~ ~

Their detective agency, the Two Tonys Search Engine in Las Cruces, had gotten three calls on Friday afternoon, not a single one over the week-end. Most likely, there would be a couple of messages waiting for them when they got back. Monday mornings were usually their busiest time of the week. With three potential new clients they would be swamped, but after a one-week hiatus they were pleased the business was picking up again.

The first call had been from Mrs. Cecilia Mendoza, who was worried about her dog and her long time helper. Both had been missing for two days. She insisted that it was not urgent as they most likely had been delayed, and that a neighbor would be helping her Monday afternoon. "Come during the beginning of the week, but not too early, around nine at the earliest," she told them. They had arrived at her house, in Silver City, at nine fifteen, after a two-hour drive from Las Cruces.

The second call was from Rick Laney, a rancher from Hillsboro, who was missing some of his freshly branded calves. He left directions to his ranch and asked them to come on Monday, but preferably after three in the afternoon, so he could get back home in time to meet them.

Max Maxwell was their last call. He had lost two of his pet geese. He had found a few goose feathers next to what he said were mountain lion tracks. He thought the other goose could still be around. He also had a friend staying with him, who might be looking for a relative or for a bear. It was hard to understand the gruff, slurred voice. He would like them to come by and talk to both of them soon.

That evening they had made plans to see all three clients during the same day. Monday, starting early, they would make a big loop, going first to Silver City, then to the Mimbres Valley to look for a missing goose and maybe someone or some other animal, and finally through the scenic Black Range Road, to the Walking 4 Ranch on the East side of Hillsboro.

~ ~ ~

The Tonys are conjoined twins of different gender, a rare oddity. They appear as a single person, slim, with strong Italian features, and a long head topped with black curly hair. Their unique body harbors a large brain, a wide chest that accommodates bigger than average blood organs and the genitalia of both genders. Except when sleeping, their thoughts rarely slowed down, as like close siblings they would often argue, worry, or jest before eventually agreeing about their common concerns. When working with their various customers,

Antonio and Antonia chose whether they would present themselves as male or female and dressed up as needed for the job.
They rarely failed in being believed to be one or the other of a
set of twins.

Most of their clients wished to find a missing relative or
to know if their spouse were cheating on them. Usually these
were matters they did not want to report to the police. This
time was different. The twins had reflected internally.

Looks like we're in the animal hunting business this week!
Except for the missing helper.
Unless she's a bigger poodle!
Funny, Sis! Think this Max is loco?
He sounded rational when we called him back. Weird about the
relative that could be a bear! Probably just wants to appraise us first.

~ ~ ~

Their first client that day was Mrs Cecilia Mendoza, a dig-
nified eighty-two year old. She shook Antonia's hand, then
directed her to a small table in the living room. She lived in
a narrow two-story brick house right on the edge of the "Big
Ditch," a steep canyon that used to be Main Street a hundred years ago, before a large flash flood had trenched its way
through town.

The petite woman held herself erect, despite the obvious
shrinkage of her body. Her still dark hair, held in a tight bun,
showed only a few white strands near her temples. Her pale
make-up of pink cheeks and lips did not hide a face that em-
anated kindness. Gold-flecked brown eyes, bordered by deep,

radiating wrinkles, widened as she smiled at Antonia, offering her a seat on a tapestry covered armchair.

"Thank you for coming, dear," she said, as she poured two cups of sweet-smelling Earl Grey tea from a steaming, delicate porcelain pot. "Sugar or milk, dear?"

Antonia was quick to reply. "Thank you, Ma'am. I prefer it straight and dark. How can I help you?"

The woman pushed toward Tony a pyramid of vanilla cookies, artfully displayed on a plate of the same fragile porcelain as the cups and tea pot.

"I have this lovely young girl working for me, five days a week. Her name is Gisela, Gisela Alvarez. On Wednesday afternoon she took Elsie, my miniature poodle, for her walk. But she did not bring her back."

With a soft napkin, she dabbed the corner of her mouth after a last bite of her cookie. She took a sip of tea and continued, "You see, dear, normally she takes Elsie with her on Friday evenings and comes back on Monday mornings. That way I don't have to take my little one for a walk. It is becoming harder for me to walk any length of time. I thought at first, that she had taken Elsie to her home in Cliff, and would be back the next day. She has done that a few times before. But she did not show up on Thursday or Friday, and now, dear, I am worried that something has happened to her or to Elsie. I have not been able to reach her on her phone. It is disconnected. She must not have paid her phone bill." Tear were welling up at the corners of the small woman's eyes.

"Mrs. Mendoza, could I have your helper's address and phone number?" Antonia asked her gently.

The older woman pulled a fine linen handkerchief out of her sleeve, and wiped her eyes. Before she got up, she picked up a microscopic fleck of cookie from her black skirt and placed it on her saucer. Then she went into a back room and returned right away, holding an address book and a stack of pictures.

"Here, dear, these are photographs of Elsie and of Gisela." She handed Antonia the stack of pictures she had already prepared. She pointed to the most recent ones. They showed a miniature black poodle, posing for the camera. The helper, Gisela, looked to be in her early twenties. She had short, dark hair, dark eyes and a look that meant to intimidate. Tony immediately tried the phone number. She confirmed it was disconnected.

"When was the last time you reached her at this number?"

Mrs. Mendoza took her time before answering. "It was probably about four weeks ago. I wanted her to pick up some milk on her way here. Her phone worked fine, at that time. We do not confer much by phone. I prefer to talk in person."

"Please, do not mind my next questions, they are part of my investigation."

The gentle lady gave her a nod, before dabbing at her eyes once more.

"Have you noticed anything missing from the house. Money, silverware, ornaments, jewelry?"

She seemed to think about it, staring at the top of some low bookshelves, filled with porcelain bibelots, then she looked around the room, before asking Antonia to follow her into a small dinning room. There, she opened the top drawer of a large, glass-cased, mahogany cabinet.

"I cannot find the serving silverware my grandmother gave me when I married. Gisela must have cleaned them and stored them somewhere else. They need to be cleaned regularly or the silver will tarnish. Since we're looking at things of value, would you mind following me into my bedroom."

She strolled to another room and went directly to a beautiful walnut cabinet, with a dozen narrow drawers. Reaching behind it, she took out a small key and fitted it into the lock near the top. She slowly pulled open the bottom drawer. Cheap colorful necklaces and bracelets. She closed it shut and exposed the next one, which contained an assortment of brooches, all lined up in a row, neatly arranged, but for two open spaces. She went to her night table and picked up a pad of paper and a set of reading glasses. A long list filled the top page with embellished cursive writing.

Sis, she already knows what's missing! Why didn't she call the cops?

Worried about the poodle!

She continued searching through all the drawers, one by one, placing checkmarks on the inventory list of missing items. She looked around the room once more, before they moved back to the living room.

"Mrs. Mendoza, you seem to already know about this theft. Why haven't you contacted the police?"

"Dear, I do not want the police to arrest Gisela. She is a good girl at heart. She is probably having a hard time at home. She helps me around the house. You have no idea, dear, how hard it is to find good help."

"Ma'am, good help does not steal from anyone, nor disappear with their pet."

Sis, is she holding the dog in coercion against calling the cops?

Told you already.

Thanks, Miss Know-it-all.

"The police would retrieve your stolen goods and they would return Elsie to you too. It may teach her not to steal from future employers anymore."

The kind lady dabbed at her eyes again, then as if wanting to convince Antonia she could deal with the situation, she said: "You see, dear, her grandmother was a close friend of mine. We went to school together. I promised her I would watch over Gisela, if she passed away before me. She passed away eight years ago, and when it became too tiring for me to do the house chores, I hired her granddaughter. Gisela started here a little over three years ago. She works four hours a day, five days a week. Something must have happened to her in the last few weeks. This is when things started disappearing, one or two at a time. The first time, I am fairly sure she took a set of Russian dolls my mother had given me when I was a child."

She pointed to an empty spot above the bookshelves. "I asked her about it and she said that she had not seen them. I thought then, that maybe she had broken the set, while cleaning it up. Then some of the older silverware went missing, the ones I only use on special occasions. After that, the jewelry I had inherited from my parents, started disappearing too. It was mostly the gold jewels; pendants, rings, and a matching bracelet and necklace from my Spanish great-grandmother. I asked her again about them. But she acted offended. Now she has Elsie.

And dear, that is the reason I do not want the police involved."

Antonia gently touched her arm, and asked: "Are you sure that no one else could have taken part or all of your missing valuables?"

"I am fairly certain that she took them, dear. I have very few visitors, maybe one a month, besides a young lady who takes my blood pressure every other week, right here in the living room. Anyone who comes to visit does not go into my chambers. Gisela is the only one who does, for dusting and cleaning only."

"Mrs. Mendoza, could you please, tell me all you know about Gisela? Her background, her attitude towards you especially recently, any conversations which might be relevant to explain this stealing of your property?"

She took a few deep breaths, dabbed her nose, and stood a little straighter in her armchair.

"Antonia dear, my good friend Anita Martinez Alvarez had three sons. When her husband Raymundo Alvarez passed away, she moved into a small apartment they owned in Silver City. She gave the farm and the land they owned in Cliff to her sons, with the prerogative that the property would belong to all three of them, and could not be divided as long as all three were alive. It is a very nice ranch, right on the Gila River. I first saw it when Anita and Raymundo were married. There were many green fields bordered with tall cottonwood trees by the river side. My husband and I stayed in their beautiful hacienda."

She poured more tea into their cups and took a sip before continuing. "Within a month after the boys inherited the property, Henrique, the youngest one suffered a shot in the face while he was cleaning his rifle. He lived for one day after he reached the hospital. Less than a year later, Big Ray, the oldest brother, his wife and their two daughters were washed away while crossing the river during a flood. Not one of them survived."

Coincidence, Sis?

Don't start, Tone. Have a nasty suspicion too. Let's see what else she has for us.

The woman carefully wiped her mouth after another sip of tea.

"So you see, dear. This only left Raul Alvarez, and his two children: young Gisela and her older brother, Ray. Their mother Marie divorced Raul, when the children were very young. After she left, he went to drinking heavily. In that little village, the local rumors were that he was violent. Cliff has grown into a small town now, but everyone still knows every other person's business. Gisela came to work once with a black eye. She finally admitted that her father had hit her. I wanted her to move out and live here in town. But she said that she had to stay home to take care of her father, so he would not drink so much."

"Thank you for sharing all of this. My brother and I will be careful, if she is at her father's ranch. Has she said anything else about her relationship with her father or if she has any monetary problems?"

"Oh dear! She always wants me to pay her in advance. I suspect that she spends it as soon as she gets it. I've tried to not give it to her all at once. Actually a month ago, I started giving her only half her pay at the beginning of the week and the rest on Fridays when she leaves. She does not like that, but that way I know she still has some money for the week-end. And by the way, I pay her by checks. I do not like to keep any cash on hand, except small amounts for home deliveries."

They talked a little longer, Antonia finished her tea before leaving, promising to keep Mrs. Mendoza informed of any development.

~ ~ ~

On the way to the Mimbres Valley, the Tonys called their friend and associate José, who had been helping them with their investigations for the last three years. As a retired police officer, he still had access to a wealth of information at his fingertips. They asked him to find out as much as he could about Gisela, her brother Ray, and their father Raul Alvarez. They described the characteristics of the Spanish gold jewelry, which seemed the most valuable and texted him the list of missing items. If he had time, they wanted him to go look at the few pawn shops and gold buyers in Silver City and find out, if he could, when was the last time Gisela cashed one of Mrs. Mendoza's checks at the Southwest Savings and Loans bank.

At a gas station on the way, the twins fueled up their Toyota truck and went inside the bathroom for a quick change into their male persona. The feminine make-up was removed. The hair was gelled and combed back to expose the forehead. They donned a striped, dark blue and white western shirt under a light canvas jacket with shoulder pads, the ubiquitous leather-belted blue jeans, a tan cowboy hat and high-heeled, light brown, riding boots. A turquoise-on-silver bolo tie dressed up the outfit. The padded shoulders, hat and riding boots made him look bigger than his sister.

~~~

Chapter Two

Birds and Lions

At la manzanita in hillsboro, as soon as Antonio finished the delicious red enchilada, the waitress was at his side.

"My mother makes this scrumptious apple pie. Would you like some for desert? With vanilla ice cream?"

"I'd love a piece of pie. Just plain, please. And a cup of coffee, dark, no sugar. Also I have a few questions about land for lease around here. Would you know someone who could help me?"

The young woman left for the kitchen. On her way, she whispered a few words to a well-padded man, wiping glassware behind the small bar. He shuffled to the Tonys' table.

"My daughter said you're looking for land in Hillsboro?"

Antonio shook his head in agreement.

"Do you mind if I sit down. I can't stand on my feet for too long."

Tony acquiesced again, as the girl brought him a cup of coffee and a large piece of warm pie.

"So, you're looking for a place in town?" The big man said, as he sat down, nudging the whole table with his generous belly, spilling some of Tony's coffee into the saucer below the cup.

"Actually, I'm looking to lease some land. Would you know of anyone willing to lease a section or two? I would like to move some cattle up to the cooler areas during the summer months. "

A smile formed on the man's face and his large middle shook the table again.

"You and a hundred more! All the private land outside town belongs to three big ranchers. And they have the BLM and the forest leases, too. There is nothing but a few acres scattered here and there, and them's for sale at a pretty high price. You'd be better off looking in Socorro County, maybe by the San Mateos. I hear you can still buy ranches over there."

Frowning slightly, Antonio continued his inquiry. "Thank you for your help. I may want to look up there. Say, I heard that one of the Laneys has a ranch up here. Is he one of the big three?"

"Yep! Second biggest. But don't waste your time. He won't let you in. He's not the friendliest guy. He's got a big ranch, so he doesn't even shop in town. My wife and his used to be friends, until she married him. Now, she don't even come to our church. She'd rather drive an hour's time than mingle with us. Know what I mean?"

"Sorry to hear that. And thanks for everything. You've been very helpful. Would you have a paper plate so I can take the rest of this wonderful pie with me?"

The pie was tasty, but a little too sweet, and would have to be savored one small bite at a time. Antonio was looking outside, through the restaurant window and through the windshield of his pick-up. It was getting warm outside. The

24

windows were slightly open, yet not enough for a Houdini dog to crawl out of. Tillie had her muzzle sticking out, panting. She needed a drink of water and a place to run. Tony shook hands with the restaurant owner and got in his truck, placing the pie to his left on the dashboard, away from the pup.

~ ~ ~

They backtracked from Hillsboro, a few miles toward Kingston, until blooming ocotillos aired their red tips and mesquite shrubs dotted the rolling slopes, their indication that the turn off to the Walking 4 Ranch was coming near. The Tonys stopped just inside the beginning of the dirt road they had been instructed would take them to the ranch in a fifteen-minute's driving distance. A weathered sign of two letters L superimposed on each other, the lower one facing backwards, followed by the words Ranch - Private Property beckoned them.

Almost looks like a swastika!

Yeah, Sis, just missing a couple of legs! Hope they don't greet us with a shotgun. What's your gut feeling?

Not making an advanced judgment. Wait and see.

They drove through the unlocvked gate and parked just a few hundred feet down the road, out of sight of the highway. They were an hour early and decided to take advantage of the extra time to give some water to Tillie, throw her a frisbee a few times, and reflect on the strange encounter with Max, their second client that morning.

~ ~ ~

Earlier, half an hour past Silver City, they had driven another dozen miles alongside the scenic Mimbres River. Towering cottonwood trees shaded its banks, bordered by green fields of short grasses, alfalfa, and fruit trees. Eventually, they arrived at a forbidding fence, with corrugated metal sheets on the bottom, chain links in the middle and finally razor wires topping the fence above eight feet, with a sign proclaiming: 'Maximus Animal Rehab Center' above the gated entrance.

Maximum detention center, Tone?

Sis, question is, once in, will we be able to leave?

They rang the bell. A chorus of dogs immediately answered. Four mutts came running to the gate. They were penned inside a narrow run that appeared to loop around the whole property. Sporting dark sunglasses and a colorful headband taming his long black hair, a tall, big-boned man came towards the gate.

"Hey! Tony Urbani, the detective, I presume?"

"You presume correctly! And you are?"

Before answering, the man opened the massive gate, let them through and shut the gate behind them.

"Maximus Maxwell. My parents were not very original. Call me Max."

Pointing at the dogs who were still in a barking frenzy, but confined to their run, he shouted. "The blind part-Rottweiler, that's Mojo. Then, that's Tammy, the three-legged retriever. Lad's the little one, old and can't hear a thing, but barks louder than the rest. And the big, drooling, Heinz 57, that's Molly. Molly's the latest, abandoned, mean and not friendly. Must have been on a short chain too long."

"Nice meeting you and your dogs, Max. My Australian

Shepherd pup is Tillie and she's going to stay in the truck."

Sitting in the driver's seat, staring at the pack, her ears down flat on the sides of her head, Tillie looked worried.

A hundred yards ahead, Max led Antonio through a pointed door, inside a large dome. Cats of all colors scattered and hid. A huge open room. All around, odd diamond-shaped windows circled the place at eye level. Up high, triangular windows brought in more light. Navajo rugs covered most of the floor. Big pillows on the rugs. Three beds along the North edge, peeked behind Chinese folding screens. An open kitchen in the back, tiled, next to a partly curtained bathroom, also tiled.

"Leave your shoes by the door or stay on the tiles"

Antonio chose to remain shod, and sat by a desk to the right of the front door.

Ready for a quick getaway, Tone?

Max stared at Antonio, who stared back at him.

Quiet, Sis. He might hear us.

On one side, with her back to the front door, a woman with long black braids was working on a narrow loom. The weaving looked half done, interspersed with sticks and feathers among rows of rust, ocher, light blue and olive green of rough, hand-spun wool. It did not show traditional patterns, but looked like a landscape, with a river snaking up it.

"This is Lenmana. She is busy right now. Needs to concentrate." The woman did not acknowledge them, but continued to work her loom.

After offering Antonio a can of beer, which he declined, the big man sat by the same table, near the door.

"So Max, tell me about these geese you're missing."

"They were a rescued pair. Canadian geese. The gander had been shot a year ago. Left wing was pretty much damaged. Couldn't fly when I got him. His mate always stayed right beside him. One of my friends found them on the edge of Bill Evans Lake. He brought them to me. Like I told you on the phone, this is an animal rescue center. We'll go look at the other animals later on. So this guy brings me these two geese in a cage. I took care of the gander. Taped his wing. He did real good. His lady was always preening him. Then one day, about three months ago, he started flying. Not too well at first. But then in the last couple of weeks, they would fly together, you know, make a couple of circles above the compound and then come right back in."

He took a long sip of his beer, looked down into the can, sighed and continued. "Then Wednesday evening, the dogs were going crazy. I had fed everyone early in the afternoon, so I went to look. Everybody seemed OK, but the geese had flown the coop. I figured they were ready to be wild again, you know. It had been getting really warm. I figured they probably found a bunch of their old friends. But then the next morning, I found his feathers not too far from the road. I found one cougar track. Just one. These mountain lions around here, don't leave much sign. I swear they walk on rocks, just so we can't track them."

He took the last sip of his beer, crushed the can and lobbed it over his head into a basket filled with more cans. "Reason I don't think she was the one to get eaten, is that I found the bad wing. It was left behind. Maybe, it did not taste right. But there wasn't enough feathers for two birds. Geese have such a thick coat, there should have been a lot of feathers, but there wasn't enough for two. So I looked and called her. But I did not find her. She's probably hiding, traumatized, you know, loosing her hubby like that, in front of her eyes."

Tone, let's look around, before the wind picks up.

"Max, could you show me where all this happened? I'd like to use my dog, if you don't mind."

"Sure! Let me grab a beer. You're sure you don't need one?"

~ ~ ~

The Rehab Center abutted the National Forest on one side. On the other side, a wild field of grasses, bushes, with a scattering of piñon and juniper trees.

"This is it. Right there! That lion track is almost gone. I had circled it. See."

There were still a lot of fine grey feathers hanging onto the brush next to the foot print. Tony had Tillie on a leash. He let her get a whiff of the goose's broken wing Max had handed him. "Find, girl. Find!"

The dog sniffed the air, sneezed, then sniffed again, and lowered her head. Tony released her from the leash. She zigzagged for a few feet, then made a bee-line for a compact Apache Plume with white flowers and pink feathery fruits, a hundred feet away. She sat down and barked once. Underneath the shrub, there was a shallow depression with flattened grasses and a couple of grey feathers.

That's her first real find. All those practice exercises are working.

Maybe lions and geese smell stronger than people.

Most people! Max is really pungent.

Antonio praised Tillie. "Good girl!" He gave her a pat on the back and handed her a treat. She swallowed it fast, looked at him, then sticking her head forward, she pointed her muzzle toward the back of the field. She was staring intently at an old adobe house standing in front of some pale rocks, a few hundred yards away. A dirt road led to it, further down the pavement.

"Max, does someone live in that house back there?"

"Yeah! That's old Randy Parker. My redneck neighbor. We don't get along. He won't go anywhere without his shotgun. He hates everything, my dogs, my donkeys, even my truck. Too much racket, he says. He's probably a hundred years old by now. I don't think he can hear anymore, so I don't know why he would care about the noise? Haven't seen him for a long while. Better that way!"

"I'd like to go and meet him, if you don't mind."

"You go by yourself, then. Thanks for finding out what happened to Jolie, my goose. She probably got carried off by that lion when he was done with her mate. I'm gonna go have another beer."

Tony followed him to get his truck.

Best to have some glass and metal between us and the old neighbor with a shotgun when we meet him!

~ ~ ~

Antonio drove to the old adobe and waited inside the truck.

After a couple of minutes, an old man opened the front

door. Long white hair struck out under a ratty straw hat, a hunting vest with gold and red shot shells popping out of bandoleer pouches, worn-out blue jeans tucked in dirty cowboy boots, he was carrying a shotgun in his left hand, as predicted. Antonio stepped out of the truck. "Hello, Mr. Parker."

The old man had the gruff voice of a habitual smoker. "Who wants to know?"

"Sir, my name is Antonio Urbani. I was hired by your neighbor to find his goose."

"Not too many Italians in these here parts."

He spat a wad of brown tobacco juice in front of him, wiped his mouth with the back of his denim sleeve and continued. "That no-good son of a gun. He gets these animals, gets money to take care of them. They even bought him the place, let him build that bowl-shaped monster. He's not from around here. He doesn't understand critters. He can't keep them dogs from barking all the time. He can't even keep the predators from eating his birds."

No neighborly love right here!

Right, Sis, but that's my cue!

It looked like the man could keep on ranting all day. Tony cut him off. "Actually, the birds are what I'm looking into. Mr Maxwell just lost his Canadian gander to a mountain lion, but it looks like the female hid and may have escaped. I was wondering if maybe you had seen her?"

The old man chuckled. "You look like a city dude, but you and your dog have a little country savvy. If you look behind the house, you'll find more goose feathers. After I heard the commotion the other night, as soon as the sun was up the next day, I went to see what that was about. That goose was under a bush, not moving. Her head was folded back. She looked like a rock. I thought she was dead. I picked her up, but she hardly put up a fight. Them birds, they mate for life. Once they loose their mate, they don't want to keep going. So I dressed her up and had me a nice goose roast. Why don't you pick up a few feathers from out back, and take them to that son of a gun, and tell him she was mighty tasty."

"Thank you for being honest, Mr. Parker. I'll let Mr. Maxwell know what happened to his goose."

"There ain't no sense in lying. It always comes back to bite you."

~ ~ ~

After picking up the few grey feathers that had not blown away, Tony went back to let Max know about the fate of his goose.

Looking sad, the big man said. "Well, at least the old bastard had a good meal."

He turned to the weaver, still at her loom. "Lenmana, what do you think?"

She was checking us out, Tone.

Good thing we followed up on the goose.

Her long dark braids twitched as her head shook a little, but the woman did not turn around. She lifted her right hand, her index finger pointing up, a wait-a-minute gesture. Methodically, she finished feeding a shuttle through the warp of her tall loom. Then using a large comb, she tightly pressed the new strand of wool down. She slowly placed the shuttle down on a low table, and finally spun her stool around, facing them. A beautiful Amerindian in her late twenties, but in her soft, tan face, the eyes were unfocused, two black pools look-ing in their direction. "I want to talk to the woman detective."

She's blind, Sis!

Max frantically gestured toward Antonio. He pointed to his eyes, then waved his index finger back and forth. Tony nodded his head to show that he understood. Meanwhile, after Lenmana took a deep breath, she continued in the same unhurried tone: "Last week, I dreamt about Mother She-bear. She was wading in a flood plain filled with filthy, brown water. She called out to a little yellow owl and his companion, a black cougar. The woman detective knows these beings. She can help me find She-bear."

Don't know what she's talking about.

More animals for us to look for, Sis?

Antonio replied: "I'll ask my sister about these animals. Can you tell me more about the she-bear?"

Lenmana turned slightly towards Max. "I will have this weaving done on Wednesday. Can we go see the woman detec-tive Wednesday afternoon?"

Max turned back to Tony. "Can she see her Wednesday?"

"Sure! Wednesday, at ten. My sister will be there."

Turning back to her loom, picking up her shuttle, Lenmana replied: "That will work. Bring me the laughing yellow owl and the black cougar."

What is she talking about, Sis?

Still don't know. Maybe we should ask Rosetta."

Antonio asked: "How do we…, I mean, how will my sister know these animals?"

Facing her loom, holding her shuttle still in her right hand,

Lenmana answered: "The little owl has a golden head and white feathered wings but cannot fly on his own. The black panther is his protector, she helps him see and fly."

Tony continued:"Black panthers are very rare, and do not live around here. Is your bear unusual too?"

While facing her loom, with impatience in her voice, she replied: "No! She is a very big black bear, with brown hair in her coat, and a little bit of white hair on her nose.

"How do I find these animals?"

Still facing her weaving, she dismissed him: "They were in my dream. Your sister will find them."

Max told them: "I'll take her to your office on Wednesday morning, then. Would you like to look at the other rescued animals?"

Already puzzled by the two people's unusual manners, the twins begged off to look at them another time, and left to make their way through the Black Range.

~ ~ ~

Chapter Three

The Walking Four Ranch

TIME TO FIND MISSING CATTLE AT THE WALKING 4 ranch. After running back and forth, chasing scents, her nose close to the ground, Tillie reluctantly got back in the pick-up.

Just as they started moving, a grey truck pulled up behind them. The round New Mexico Livestock Board logo was printed on the door. A stocky brunette in a grey uniform jumped out. "Hi, I'm Martha Laney. My father called you about his calves," she said as she shook hands with Antonio through the open truck window.

"Yes, Ma'am. Tony Urbani, with Two Tonys Search Engine."

"Thanks for coming. My father is eager to meet you. I'll lead the way to the ranch. It can be a little tricky at first, not knowing which dirt road to take."

They followed her truck up and down hills, over twisting, narrow roads, glad that they would not need to guess which way to go. Occasionally, a bunch of black cattle dotted the landscape.

After a mile of churning road dust, a huge, red-roofed hacienda stood in the middle of an open field of wild grasses. Behind it, on one side, two horses were prancing inside a large corral, next to a barn filled with hay. On the other side, against a rising hill, a giant, silver, quonset hut. Through the wide open doors, heavy equipment could be seen.

As they pulled up in front of the house, a pack of barking dogs, all blue Queensland heelers, rushed to the pickup. Answering them from a series of long chain-link pens, half a dozen hounds were baying, jumping up and down. A white dually pickup drove out of the equipment shed towards the house. A tall man stepped out of the truck extending his hand to Tony. He was dressed in full cowboy regalia: tan, buffed bullhide boots; an oval silver buckle belted over creased and ironed blue jeans; pearl snaps on a western shirt with a silver bolo tie in the shape of a bucking horse; the whole topped by a white, large-brimmed hat that he had to take off for a second to step out of his truck. He called off the dogs as he walked toward Tony, his sun-weathered face smiling. "Good afternoon. I'm Rick Laney. Thank you for coming."

He lead Antonio to the house, through a screened porch, into a large living room filled with southwestern furniture. Oil paintings of cowboy scenes adorned the white walls. The smell of warmed cinnamon permeated the room. Waving toward a short, red-haired woman wearing an apron, Mr. Laney introduced her, "My wife, Mary Lou. She can bring us coffee, if you'd like."

"Thank you, ma'am. My name is Tony Urbani. Pleased to meet you. I just finished drinking a cup of coffee at La Manzanita. But, if I could I trouble you for a glass of water, please, I'd truly appreciate. It's a scorcher outside, today."

As soon as the woman had turned around, Rick Laney went straight to business. "Rick junior is fixing the backhoe. He'll join us in a while. I see you've met my daughter, Marsha. I don't know what William is doing. Never there when I need him." There was a touch of bitterness in his voice.

"And William is?" Tony inquired.

"My youngest son. He would like to run the ranch, but is not interested in cattle. He likes to be on horseback, and he's a good roper, but in general, he prefers drinking beer with his buddies.

"You're talking about me, father?" A thirty-some-year-old version of his dad, but for a red mane sticking out of a ball-cap advertising a brand of beer, walked in from the kitchen, followed by his mother, who was carrying a plateful of still-steaming, glazed cinnamon buns and a pitcher of water. "Hi, I'm Bill, or William, the wayward son," he continued, staring at his father. Then, he shook hands with Tony, trying to crush his hand in the process. But Antonio was ready, and returned the favor until he saw the red-haired man wince a little. Martha was watching. She let out a short laugh. "Hah! Tony is on to you."

The father took over. "All right, children. Enough games. Let's get down to the problem at hand. Tony, as I mentioned on the phone, I have been missing some cattle at regular intervals. It started three years ago. It seems that right after we brand, half a dozen calves end up missing. It's usually the older calves in the bunch, a couple of months old. We do have a few large predators: lions, bears, coyotes, even the occasional re-intro-duced wolf. But for the wolves, the usual predators don't usually go after the newborn calves. There are easier preys. They also prefer the ones who haven't had their shots yet. The unusual aspect about these disappearances is that it happens right after we work them. Within a week or two. You see, when most of the calves are about a month old, we give them a blackleg shot, earmarks: a slanted cut on the left; and an ear tag on the right: an orange, numbered, plastic tag. Then they get a very fresh 'Walking 4' brand on their left shoulder. The last ones that went missing were around two months old. The ones that were born early, the bigger ones. This is becoming very costly. We ride many days after the branding, checking our fences, looking at signs, and asking our neighbors, with no success. My daughter and the other livestock inspectors in the state have been on the look-out for them. They haven't discovered anything so far. I hope you can find out what happened to them."

As they sat down around the large dining table, another man walked in. A younger, spitting image of Rick, with the same dark hair. The twins did not miss the look of hatred William shot at his brother, who completely ignored him. "Hello. I'm Richard the third. Pleased to meet you," he said as he sat down with them.

"If you don't need me?" The mother said, not waiting for an answer, as she went back into the kitchen.

Richard the third, looked about ten years older than William. Their father nodded toward Richard, obviously a signal they had previously agreed on. "As my father probably mentioned to you, the next couple of days after branding, my brother and I ride the pasture we leave them in. We make certain they have 'mammied' up. That they are back with their mother, you see. After that, we work the waters, the fences, and anything else needs

38

fixing on the ranch. We go back to check on them a week or two later, and that's when we find the cows balling for their calves. About five or six of them, each time! I don't know how much you know about ranching, but one or two could succumb to the big predators we have around here, but six is too many for any mountain lion or pack of wolves to kill at once without leaving a trace. Even a big lion and her kits."

While Rick Junior took a deep breath, turning to the father, Antonio grabbed the opportunity to answer. "Sir, although I live in the city, I've helped a few friends with their cattle. I have a few questions."

Bill barged in. "So who did you work for? Which rancher?"

The father snapped at his son: "William, be civil, please."

Hostile brat, Tone.

But nice-looking!

Don't be so shallow.

Tony chose to ignore Bill, and continued: "How often do you brand or work your herd?"

The older brother responded, "We have four herds, each a little over a hundred heads, mother cows and bulls, in separate pastures. We run a cow-calf operation. Angus on Limousins. We usually brand in May and June and then again in late July or August. Then we gather for sales in November and again in February. We don't have set dates. We brand when most of the calves are about a month old, and we sell according to the market and our buyers. For the last two years, we have made sure we didn't brand on the same dates as the years before."

"Who would know when you brand?"

Again Rick Junior was the one answering. "Tom and Larry

Gilman, our neighbors on the north-east side. We take turns working for each other. We use the same cowboys. We've known all of them for years. Locals and trustworthy, I'm certain. Isn't that so, Father?"

The older Rick nodded, and said: "I've known Juan and Sam Carrillo for years. They both live at the Gilmans. Father and son. Good Christians. Good people. As for Ron and David Morones, I've helped raise these two brothers. I've put them on horseback when they were four years old. Their father lived at the ranch when my dad ran it. When we're short-handed, we also use the Parras. They help everybody around here, when they're not training kids for rodeos."

"Thank you, sir. I'd like to get everyone's contact info, if possible. Were there others who have helped you in the past?"

"Not since I've been running the ranch! Thirty plus years now. We don't care for anyone else to know our business. Marsha can tell you about the locals," the father replied.

The daughter leaned forward and replied, "I'll give you their addresses and phone numbers. I inspect all the cattle in this district. I cover all of this county and some of the adjacent areas. But our brand would be difficult to hide, when it's so fresh. They would also have to remove the ear-tags, that would leave a hole. And our earmark would still show. I've given the calves' description to the other livestock inspectors in the state, so I think it would be difficult for them to slip past one of us."

"Thank you, Marsha. Do let me know your brand and earmark." Turning back to Rick Senior, Tony asked, "You mentioned four different herds. Can you tell me how these are different?"

Rick Junior took over again, "One herd is registered, the other three are commercial. We raise 'Lim-flex'. Limousin cows crossed on Angus bulls, you see. Our registered herd is straight Angus. Except for this last time, half of the calves that went missing have been from our best commercial herd. The registered cattle are sold at specialized auctions. We sell directly to the middleman our heifers and steers from the other three herds. It's almost as if the thieves know which calves to take."

The older man immediately replied: "Now son, we do not know for certain that these are being stolen. That's why we're hiring Mr. Urbani, here."

William snorted and cut in: "Father, I can find out who's stealing the calves. Please, let me do it, rather than have this fancy dude look for them."

Ouch! You look too slick, Tone.

Rick Senior had a stern look on his face. "William, your manners, please! You tried once and failed. Let a professional do it this time." Then, turning to Antonio "Forgive my son, Mr. Urbani. He is as upset as we all are about this."

The younger Richard started again, "Last month, my brother spent a few nights with the cattle, right after our last branding. A week later, six of our registered calves went missing. We still don't know what happened to them. Now, if you don't have any more questions for me, I'm going back to work."

"One more quick question, if you don't mind?"

Rick Junior nodded. Then hesitantly, not knowing if the subject was going to offend them, Tony asked. "Did you,... or have you run across any cattle mutilations or other unexplained surgery done to your cattle, in the last few years?"

The younger Rick smiled for the first time. "We have not!

But down south, by Deming, there has been reports of strange cattle mutilations. But that was at least twenty years ago. Now, Father, could you help me when you're done here? I should be ready to put the bucket back on the backhoe in fifteen minutes."

Rick acquiesced. His son turned back toward Tony as he was leaving. "Pleasure meeting you. Call me anytime, if you have more questions."

"Pleasure's mine. Thank you for your expertise."

Tony did have more questions. He asked, "Do you tattoo their ears?"

Bill snorted: "What for? Who's going to get close enough to check their ears?"

The older Rick said, "We do not. It takes extra time to add a tattoo to each calf. We want to have them back to their mothers as soon as possible. Although, that may be the way we need to go, at least for the registered herd. You see, we thought the numbered ear-tags and our brand would be enough."

Bill interjected, "We'll be branding all night, if we have to ink their ears. That's the stupidest thing I've ever heard."

Rick frowned and replied: "No, William. Manners, please. The Gilmans do it. Once you get used to it, it only takes a few more seconds for each calf."

Tony continued: "Although it would be expensive, time consuming, and it may not work over long distances, have you considered radio frequency chip implanting?"

Bill interjected: "Father, you know these RFID only work in corrals or flat land, not in the hills. I've found their tracks before, I can find them again. I'm sure this city detective has never tracked a cow or a horse before."

Tony answered: "Actually, William, my sister and I joined Search and Rescue a few years back. It's a great volunteer organization, and that first year, one of the Las Cruces teams offered a tracking training with the help of an excellent professional tracker. We trained every week-end for three months. After that, we've kept up with our skills whenever we go outside of town. Of course, I'm sure I'm not as experienced as you are. But tell me, what kind, and where were those tracks you found?"

Smooth move, Fancy Dude!

Bill was quiet for a minute. "That was a couple of year ago. I found drag marks by the fence on the East end of the Lower Animas pasture. I thought they had roped a calf and drug it to the other side of the fence. The fence had been cut and repaired right there. And there were a few vehicle tracks on the other side of the fence, right on the dirt road near it."

Tony wanted to know when they would brand again.

Rick Senior explained: "We last branded the Long-Bottom pasture two weeks ago. That pasture borders two county dirt roads. We've never lost calves from there. Then we'll brand the late-born in August, in all four pastures. Should not be too many calves."

"So, if I wanted to ride the ranch's fences, can I drive all around or would I need a horse?"

William loudly blew out his cheeks in disapproval. Rick gave his son a menacing look before replying: "There are not that many roads in the Northern pastures. Lots of hills. Horseback would be your best bet for those, unless you stay near the fences. Most of the lower pastures can be seen from a truck."

"I may want to stay near the fences. Otherwise, would you have: a gentle horse for me to ride; a good set of maps showing fences, water holes and gates; and the dates, numbers and description of the missing calves." Tony asked.

Rick Senior told his son, "William, get me the six topo maps that are on top of my desk." Then turning to his daughter, "Marsha, please, give to Mr. Urbani the list of names and numbers of everyone who has helped us." At last, he looked at Tony: "I'll have a gentle horse bridled on the days you want to ride. Do you have your own saddle?"

Tony did not. Rick told him that he would loan him a Western saddle, and to just let him know when he would be coming over to ride.

"First, I'd like to look at that area William mentioned in the Lower Animas pasture. It will be three or four days before I can come by. I'll give you a call before-hand. We have a couple of other clients needing help at the moment. But we will start working on it right away from the office." Tony said, as he collected the maps and the contact numbers from the two siblings.

They all shook hands. As he was leaving, again Bill tried to crush his hand, but Tony got the best of him.

Don't like him, he's a creep!

He's just insecure, Sis, the baby of the family.

You're too soft, Tone. Watch out for him.

Sure, but he is kind of cute with that bright red hair.

~ ~ ~

44

Chapter 4
Juggling Cases

THAT EVENING, WHEN THE TONYS FINALLY GOT back to Las Cruces, José was waiting for them in the office. For dinner, with what he could find in the fridge, Antonio fixed a large salad, a raspberry vinaigrette and a tray of cheese, before they sat down at the kitchen counter.

While munching on corn chips, guacamole and kalamata olives, José handed Tony a few sheets of paper. Although he relied on electronic input like everyone else, he was born in the age of pen-and-paper, most of his notes were handwritten. An old-fashioned gumshoe, he also believed in personal contact to get information, allowing him to better assess the people he connected with.

"Here is what I found about the Alvarez. Not much on Gisela, mostly her high school records. She was an average student. She worked as a waitress for six months, at El Pollo Loco in Silver City. Applied for and received food stamps after she quit the restaurant. No record of any work for the last five years. I guess that is about the time she started helping Mrs. Mendoza."

He stopped and took another bite before continuing, "Now, her brother Ray has a completely different story. He also went to the Cliff High School, then for one year at WNMU in Silver City. No records of jobs after school. Busted a few times for fighting and petty thievery. I talked to a friend who works as a deputy for the county, she told me that the kid is a suspected meth producer but they had not been able to find his lab. Last year, her and her boss went to old man Raul's, Gisela's father, looking for Ray, but he greeted them with a 30-30 and told them to get out of there. This was his place and he did not know where his: quote 'worthless son-of-a-bitch kid' was, but that the boy did not live with him. Raul, or Ralo as he is known in Cliff, has a bad reputation in town. He is a violent drunk, starts fights with anyone, usually ends up getting beat up enough to go to the hospital, and then takes the other person to court for attacking an old, crippled 'Nam vet'. He has gotten quite a few of his opponents to pay for his medical bills. Of course, it helps that the judge is related to him. It might also explain why they can't get a warrant to search his place. He has a few priors. Two 'driving under the influence', and three 'driving without a license'. His maximum jail time has been three days at a time. Then he is out, usually under surveillance in a local hospital, before he is free to go home, with a slap on the wrist. Sheriff's deputy says he still drives, but they haven't caught him in the last few years." He finished before he attacked his salad.

"Thank you, José." Antonia replied in her melodious voice.

The twins did not hide their duality to José, as he had discovered it a few years before. His help had proven invaluable, moreover he insisted on working pro bono for them. They only covered his expenses. He claimed that as a retiree from the police force, he would perish of boredom if not for helping them.

Antonio took over. "Did you have a chance to visit the local pawn shops?"

"I went to see a couple of them, including a small one in Cliff. Without pictures of the missing jewelry, it has been difficult to get answers from the owners. Do you think Mrs. Mendoza would talk to me?"

Antonia replied "We can ask her. I think she will be agreeable to a meeting. She speaks a very proper English. I have a feeling it would be best not to speak Spanish with her."

"I do respect your intuition, and will follow your directives. Can you get me an appointment with her, please."

Antonia told him she would call Mrs. Mendoza in the morning.

José mentioned how he had looked up Maximillian Maxwell, as well. Born in California forty-five years before, he went for two years of college in animal husbandry, before immersing himself in the various native American cultures. Ten years ago, Max, using a Diné name, was caught replicating Navajo artwork he sold as genuine artifacts. His defense was that being a sixty-fourth native American, he thought he was entitled to use his heritage, although he had no record of his alleged Cherokee lineage.

The Tonys gave José a list of the cowboys who had helped the Laneys and asked him to find out what he could about them. After finishing dinner, they discussed their strategies a little longer for the various cases, before José bid them a good night and went home.

~ ~ ~

The following morning Antonio responded to the previous day's messages. The first one had been from a woman who thought her husband wanted to kill her. When they called her back, Mrs. Hunter told them that she had been mistaken, and that actually her husband was taking very good care of her. He had just given her a pearl necklace. "It's beautiful, sweetie," she had said to someone near her before she hung up.

The second one was from JR, a friend and a high-up officer of the New Mexico State Police they had worked with in the past. When Antonio reached him, JR told them he was very busy that morning and would call them later.

Then, the twins pored over the Walking Four maps and made phone calls to the Gilmans, the Laneys' neighbors. Everyone seemed genuinely concerned and offered their help.

They also called their friend Rosetta. Madame Rosetta LaFleur is a gifted medium they often used when unable to find traditional intelligence for some of their cases. She had been for many years and still was one of their vital assets, at times putting them under hypnosis to discover missing clues. She picked up the phone on the sixth ring. They considered themselves lucky, as they knew she did not believe in answering machines and rarely bothered answering her calls.

"We have a weird case on our hands. A native American

wants us to consult a laughing yellow owl and a black panther to find a big bear! Do you have any idea what she is talking about?"

Rosetta let out a big laugh. "I don't know who the missing bear is. But as you know, Mora has been studying with me. She wants to be a seer, so she can help people. She is the black panther. Now, she in turn, has taken under her wing the care of one of your mother's pupils, a young child she calls Osito, little bear, or sometimes Tecolote, the owl. Osito had Mexican parents, but has yellow hair and a light complexion. He does not talk, but laughs all the time. Maybe the woman can find the bigger bear through both of them."

"We met a young boy who smiles all the time at our mother's school. Different name, but it could be the same child. You're amazing, Rosetta. Thank you. We may have to bring Lenmana, the woman, to you, if you don't mind."

"You know I don't mind, but you'll be surprised how advanced Mora is now. Try her out. Also, I saw that you need to be careful of an old army man who has a bad temper, a proclivity for dangerous things and a taste for young boys. Just be careful in general. And I miss seeing you two. Come see me just to visit."

A few years back, the twins had rescued Mora from a pedophile ring when she was eleven years old. They had stayed in touch with the intelligent sixteen year old adolescent, whose green eyes were accented by her café-au-lait complexion. For the last three years, she had been attending the Tonys' mother's college: Angel Imelda's School for the Gifted.

Mora now spoke fluently four different languages, and was getting proficient in Japanese. She excelled in music and science and tutored a couple of young students in Spanish, right at the school. Mora had received praises in the local news media, which had brought her nation-wide attention, attention that she shunned. Shortly after she had been invited to join two famous universities. But she had declined these, preferring to stay close to her parents and her friends at the school.

~ ~ ~

The twins' mother, Sirena, had come into an unexpected inheritance a few years back, and she had started her school for gifted and handicapped children. Grants, donations and high tuitions from those who could afford it, soon made the college very attractive with its unusual courses and extremely small student-to-teacher ratio. She had turned down many paying prospects, as she insisted in keeping it small-scaled and available to disadvantaged children.

Next the Tonys called their mother. "Mom, is a blond child named Osito still going to your school?" Antonia asked her.

"Yes, you know him. His actual name is Angel Torres. Mora calls him Osito," she replied. "What's going on?"

"We're trying to find someone or something for one of our clients. She said that we would need the help of Mora and Angel."

"I don't think Angel's mother would let him be away from the school or from her home. If you remember, Angel has Angelman's syndrome. You met his mother Janice Torres, and you now she is very protective of him, for good reasons. But I'll talk to her and maybe your client can come to the school."

50

Sirena called back a few minutes later to let them know that they could bring their client to the school, with the stipulations that Mora and Angel's mother would be present at all times during the interview, and that should the child get excited, the meeting would stop immediately.

At times, it seemed that while working on some cases, they spent most of their days on the phone or on the internet. Antonia called Mrs. Mendoza, to ask her if she had any pictures of the missing jewelry, which she had. It was an old photograph of her mother, wearing her precious gold necklace. She would need the picture back, as it was the only one she had of her mother. Antonia replied that she would send José, one of their investigators, the following day. He would make a copy, and return the picture right away.

Then Antonio called Rick Laney and asked if he could ride or drive the Lower Animas pasture of the Walking Four, this coming Saturday. The rancher told him that his son William would drive him around the ranch.

Later that evening, JR called to let them know that he would be in Las Cruces the next day, and that he had a problem he needed to attend to, but that professionally, he could no longer research. He wanted their discreet help as soon as they were available. Antonio invited him to come have dinner Wednesday evening. He replied that he would like that, and that he would bring dinner for a change. It was his turn to feed them.

~ ~ ~

Chapter 5

A Gifted Angel

By TUESDAY EVENING, JOSÉ HAD BEEN ABLE TO contact everyone working for the Laneys, except for the Parras. Antonio called them at six in the morning on Wednesday. Politely, Jesus Parra told him that they had not helped the Laneys in the last two years as they were very busy with 4H livestock and teaching roping, barrel racing and bronc riding to a dozen young kids. They thought Richard Senior and Rick Junior were doing a great job running the ranch, and they would always find the time to help them, if they were needed.

After a quick breakfast, the twins took Tillie for a long walk to the Rio Grande's edge. The dog went for a swim, then started chasing a couple of ducks to the middle of the shallow, slow-flowing river before they called her back. On the shore, she ran around in circles until the Tonys, tired of watching her, decided to go home.

Shortly after ten, Max and Lenmana arrived at the office. She wore a colorful beaded top over a mid-calf black velour skirt. Her shoes were traditional, high-laced moccasins. Two long, shiny, black braids ran down her back. She was using a wooden cane with a carved white crane head in her left hand, with which she barely touched the floor in a narrow side to side motion. Max was wearing his usual, slightly raunchy, Indian cowboy outfit: well-worn, crumpled, dark, tall leather boots, faded blue jeans, dark blue denim shirt with pearl snaps, the two top buttons undone, showing a tan that did not stop at the neck, complete with a tall, black, cowboy hat.

After helping her to a seat by the large desk in the twins' office, Max asked Antonia that he be texted when Lenmana was ready to be picked up. He was going to do some shopping.

For beer, no doubt!

Careful, Tone.

Speaking slowly, Lenmana said: "Max drinks a lot, but he is a good person."

She can hear us, Sis.

Smiling, Max tapped the rim of his tall cowboy hat and nodded at both women before leaving the office.

From a corner of the room, Tillie slowly and quietly moved toward the blind woman sitting by the desk. She knew she was not supposed to be near the clients, as some did not care for pets. Antonia gave her the "bad dog" stare. She stopped and peered at her human, showing her teeth in a smile, as when she knew she had done something wrong. As soon as Tony had taken her eyes off her, Tillie continued her slow progress, until she was a few inches from the woman's leg. Lenmana bent down and gave her a pat on the head, then turning toward Antonia, she said: "I can smell her. She smells friendly and nice. She is not bothering me."

Tillie responded by beating her long tail rhythmically, on the floor.

"Shall we get started then?" Antonia asked.

"Yes! Were you able to contact the laughing yellow owl and the black panther?"

Irritated by the way the woman was directing the conversation, Antonio blurted internally to his sister:

Enough with her strange demands!

Shush Tone! She can hear us. And Angel-Osito is real!

"We located both the black panther and the yellow owl, but they are not able to come here. We will try to make an appointment to see both of them today. But first, could you tell me what is going on. Why do you need us or the children?"

The blind woman leaned forward and placed her elbows on the desk, seemingly staring at Antonia. In the same slow, monotonous voice she had used at Max's dome, she started. "My mother has been missing for three months. Her name is Honaw Nez Begay, but all her children call her Honey. She is a Nádleehí, a two-spirit person." She stopped as if waiting for a response.

Antonia said: "That is a person born in one gender, but who functions as the other gender. Is that correct?"

"Correct!" Lenmana smiled, glad that she would be understood. "My mother was born in the male form, but from the age of three, she knew she was a woman. When she was twelve years old, she had a vision and changed her identity. Except for a few outside city dwellers, my people respect her very much. She adopted me and many other children. Honey has many visions and seeks to improve the world we live in." She paused for a minute.

So her mother is a guy?

Enough, Tone.

Antonia offered Lenmana a glass of water, but she declined it, and continued. "I do not like your brother. Honaw is a mother-bear. She is concerned about the current state of the plants and the animals in this country. She hears the cries of living things who are suffering and dying of sickness today. Five months ago, she went on a trip to the East side of the state, where she saw horrible damage done to cattle and hogs. She came back to Nageezi for one week. She was very depressed, because she could not help them. Then, Mother Honaw left for the southern part of New Mexico. She wanted to see how the cattle factories functioned down there. I have not seen my mother since she left, three months ago. One of my uncles reported he had heard that she had an accident near Magdalena, shortly after she left. My uncle helped me find the place where someone ran her over on her bicycle. We could not find out much from the people near there. Only that her bicycle was completely destroyed and that she did not want any medical help. When they saw her last, she was walking on the road to the South. While I sat in my uncle's car, near where she had the accident, I saw a she-bear walking south through the big forest. My uncle took me to our friend Max. His place is at the southern end of the Gila National Forest. Two weeks ago, I saw Mother Honaw again and she told me to look for the little yellow laughing owl and his companion the black panther. When can we go see the yellow owl?"

How can she see all that with her condition, Sis.

Lenmana answered: "Your brother is very rude. I see inside my head. I see in my dreams. Can you call the yellow owl, right away?"

Sorry, Sis, but she's rude too.

Antonia tried to deflect the ambiguous squabble. "Did anyone search around the accident scene and in Nageezi?"

"The tribal police has been looking for Mother Honaw at home. She is an important person there, she is a clan chief. But they haven't found her. After the accident was reported, the police in Magdalena asked the Search and Rescue team to look for her. They searched for two days. The Farmington City Police searched the places Mother Honaw shops at. Please, would you mind calling the yellow owl?"

Antonia asked her for Honaw's physical description, and for her mother's state of mind when she last saw her. Antonio grunted internally, but kept quiet, while Lenmana talked. She described a tall, big boned, beautiful woman, with long hair she usually kept braided. She wore a small-brimmed black hat on her head and black pants under her skirt to better ride her bicycle. She carried her belongings in a backpack that many of her children had embroidered. When she left she was eager to go south, to gather plants for her medicine cabinet.

Antonia thanked her for the details. "I must warn you that Angel, the little yellow owl, is twelve years old. He is a handicapped child with limited communication and coordination skills."

Lenmana replied, "I must see him. That is what my dream showed me."

Tony called her mother Sirena for an appointment to see Angel and Mora.

She called right back, and let her know that the children could see her and her client at two o'clock that afternoon. Max came back and took Lenmana for lunch.

56

Learn to be quiet when we're talking with clients.

Most of them cannot hear us, Sis. This whole ex-male mother-bear is just too weird.

Simply part of her culture.

~ ~ ~

When Antonia first met Angel, two years before, his mother had mentioned how her eighth and last adopted boy was different.

"My Angel had a difficult start. His birth parents are both Hispanic, with dark eyes and black hair. They were not ready for this light-complected, blue-eyed, blond-haired child who would not suckle and did not express himself as other babies do. DNA tests showed that Ricardo, that is what they named him, was their child, but was afflicted with Angelman Syndrome. The hospital bills mounted rapidly and they could not pay them. Not being wealthy, they divorced, may God help them, and put him up for adoption."

Mrs. Torres had made the sign of the cross swiftly over her face and shoulders, before continuing. "New Mexico Social Services knew my husband and I adopted young boys. They told us they would cover the hospital bills already incurred if we took him in. We did. It was difficult at first, but the Lord gave us an angel, this beautiful smiling angel, so we can further his work on earth. Soon enough with love and prayers, this beautiful boy stopped having seizures and started smiling all the time. That is why we changed his name to Angel when he became part of our family."

~ ~ ~

The twins arrived early at Angel Imelda's School for the Gifted. The school was named for a young handicapped girl who was murdered a few years back. An inheritance from Sirena's deceased husband, a large anonymous donation and a few generous grants had enabled her to buy thirty acres of land west of Las Cruces, and build a school for handicapped, disadvantaged and gifted children, as well as a house for adolescent women in trouble. The adobe buildings stood above a wide, arid valley, which flooded during the summer monsoons, and were surrounded by soft rolling hills. A deep well, solar-powered, provided pure water for the school, a few farm animals, and a large garden. Grants continued to arrive, enabling the school to provide income for instructors of diverse small classes. Sirena dreamed for the school to eventually become self-sufficient.

A couple of horses and a half-dozen milk goats were moved away from the main gate by two sheepdogs, as the twins drove inside the compound. A couple of hundred yards away, in contrast with the thirsty surroundings, young people tended green plants and fruit trees inside a large, fenced-in garden. The rains would be welcomed if they came soon. Antonia stopped in the large parking lot, that stood between two major buildings and was greeted by her mother: a tall, graceful, grey-haired woman with a generous hug. Tillie went to play with the sheepdogs. Sirena mentioned how both Angel and Mora were doing so well together, how the boy was really improving with his walking and communication skills, before Antonia walked back to the gate, to wait for her clients.

Max and Lenmana arrived promptly just before two. After closing the gate behind them, Antonia guided them to the handicapped parking spot, near the school's main entrance. Her mother warmly greeted them at the door.

After noting that Lenmana was well in-hand, Max asked Sirena if he could go see the animals. After he left, the three of them moved to a large meeting room, with a half-circle of large windows facing the gardens.

One favorable point for Max, Sis.

She did not bother answering him and instead sent him a mental fog cloud.

By barely holding the blind woman by the elbow, as she had seen Max do, Antonia guided Lenmana to a comfortable armchair Sirena had pointed to. All the chairs were made of different material, shape and color, arranged in a circle.

Sirena introduced everyone to Lenmana. She first presented Angel's mother, Mrs. Janice Torres, a stout Hispanic woman in her fifties, sitting in a straight-back, wooden chair, mentioning that she was a massage therapist at the school.

Then a young school nurse who had recently joined the college. A stern-looking social worker, friend of Mrs. Torres, was also in attendance. Angel sat on the wood floor, both legs folded to one side, next to a large, red, plastic tricycle without pedals. Reddish-blond hair framed his soft, pale face. His blue eyes danced as he looked at the surrounding people. Calmly standing next to him, Mora, a graceful sixteen year old, with dark skin and finely braided black hair, made for an acute contrast to the compact, fidgety boy.

When Angel spotted Antonia, he carefully straddled his trike and walked it quickly over to her. He stopped by planting both feet firmly on the ground, almost knocking her over.

"Be careful, son," his mother told him from across the room.

He backed up his scooter and with a big smile, he shuffled a couple of wobbly steps over and grabbed Antonia's thigh in a fierce hug. His way of showing her, he liked her, just like every time he saw her.

Once everyone was settled in, Angel back on the floor in the middle of the room straddling his red scooter, Antonia started.

"We are here because Lenmana needs to find her mother Honaw, who has been missing for more than three months. In her dreams, she saw Angel and Mora. She believes that they may have information about the whereabouts of her mother."

Janice Torres spoke up. "Just so everyone understands, I will not let my Angel get upset. It takes him hours to calm down, and too much excitement could lead to a seizure. So everyone must understand that I will stop this session, if it interferes with his health."

Lenmana answered that she understood.

Mora explained that she was only a translator for the boy, and that she had been working with him for the last couple of years.

Mrs. Torres stepped in: "Mora has really improved Angel's means of communication in the last three years. With the program she created and installed on his tablet, he can communicate with all of us. We were under the impression that he did not understand most of what we told him. But we were wrong, and Mora showed us how we can interact with my Angel all the time. She really has a knack for understanding him. She is also working with him with music. He loves to play the piano. God is merciful."

Sensing that all eyes were on him, Angel crawled off his tricycle, then precariously standing up, he moved toward Lenmana, his arms raised up to the side, waving. His hands reached for her leg while he displayed a big drooling grin. The woman did not flinch when he bumped into her, nor at his touch, but her hand stretched out to his head. She felt his face, something he let few people do. Then, she ruffled his hair and said: "Can you tell me where my mother is?"

The boy just looked at her and continued to smile. He touched her velour dress and laughed. He stuck his tongue on her skirt as if tasting it, then he reached for the beads on her vest and tried to pull them off. Shaking, he lowered himself and drooling over her feet, he tried to untie the leather lace of her moccasin. His mother called him back.

Angel turned around and slowly plodded toward Mora. He patted the front of his scooter. The girl was holding a small computer, which she secured to the front of the tricycle with velcro, and turned it on. Pictures of foods and drinks near the top, a bathtub, a toilet, a chair, a bed, and many other household items were first displayed. Angel straddled his trike, laughed, then slowly but carefully, he swiped the screen sideways, right to left. Another page appeared with various foods. Still laughing, he gently swiped the tablet again. Animals and plants on the next page. Without touching the screen, the child was shaking his finger above the picture of a bear.

"A bear, Osito? You're showing me a bear," said Mora.

The boy laughed again and shook his hands. Mora asked Lenmana if that meant anything.

"Yes, it does! My mother is a she-bear. We belong to the Yellow Mud Bear clan. What else can the laughing owl tell me?"

Angel swiped his laptop and translated by Mora, he pointed to a bicycle, then to a road, then to cows. At once, he stopped smiling, got off his scooter and laid his head down on the floor, as if listening to the ground. Everyone in the room was quietly watching him. Mora walked to him, and she gently touched his shoulder. He shuddered and getting back on his trike he touched the computer. A man. A bear. A picture of Casper, the cartoon ghost. A picture of a rock. He touched the bear picture again. He started shaking his hands spasmodically as he pointed to the various pictures. Then he was hitting his head with his fists. He fell off his scooter and kept pounding his head.

Mora reached out to him. "OK, Osito. I see it. All right. I got it. Thank you, Osito. Now please, calm down." She hugged him tight, rubbing his back, until Janice sat down on the floor next to them and took her turn holding him, while massaging his shoulders and his head.

Sirena told everyone that this was enough for today. That Angel needed to rest now. She went to get apple juice, his favorite drink. His mother told him that she would draw him a nice warm bath. He looked up at her and smiled his gap-toothed smile. After he drank his juice, Janice took him away to his favorite pastime: playing in the water.

Everyone in the room relaxed as soon as the child left the room. Lenmana apologized for upsetting the boy.

Mora took the floor. "I think he's going to be fine. He loves bathing and swimming." She took a sip of her apple juice. "What I believe Osito was telling us, is that someone on a bicycle rode on a long road to see some cows. Then later a bear talked to a man. Then that man hit the bear with a rock. I don't know what Casper the ghost means. Once before, he had pointed at that picture when he wanted to watch cartoons. I don't think that's what he meant this time. But his brain was moving too fast, by then. I could not follow him. When Osito, I mean Angel, started shaking, I think he was feeling the hit on his head that the bear suffered. When he is feeling better, I will ask if I read him correctly. But that is all I can sense for today."

Antonia and Lenmana thanked Mora for her help, while Sirena went to look for Max.

~~~

After a short stop back at the office, Lenmana explained that Honaw went to look at the CAFOs in the East part of the state at first, and had mentioned that she had wanted to check on the CAFOs near the Mexican border as well, and also to gather certain medicinal plants that only grow in that area.

"By CAFO, you mean Concentrated Animal Feeding Operations?"

The blind woman answered: "Yes, that is what she went to

look at before in the eastern part of the state. She is extremely concerned that the animals are suffering in these milk and meat factories. I will try to visualize Mother Honaw in my dreams. I will talk to my uncle and to my grandmother to see if they have more suggestions for finding her. And just so you know, Mother Honaw can see ghosts. It was interesting that Master Angel saw that cartoon ghost. Maybe his young helper can talk to him when he feels better. I'll be back to see you early next week, if you can arrange another meeting with Master Angel then?"

"I will ask his mother for a Monday morning meeting and let you know."

Max had been quietly sitting by the entrance, looking at a Navajo rug in earthen colors and a couple of reproductions of Georgia O'Keefe's paintings on the opposite wall. Lenmana turned toward him and asked to be taken home.

So Sis, these seeing dreams of hers are just deductions from what her uncle has told her.

No, she has visions, maybe in her dreams, but they are real in her mind, maybe this is what she senses. She is very close to her mother.

You mean her father?

Two spirit people, Tone. Respect that. She said Honey adopted her, not birthed her. She sounds like a wise person.

Or a crazy one?

~ ~ ~

Chapter 6

Yet Another Case

JR, ALWAYS PROMPT, RANG THE BELL AT SIX o'clock, and shook hands with Antonio. He was carrying a cooler, a brown paper sack and a large bouquet of sweet-smelling pink and white lilies. "For your sister!"

"Thanks, JR. She loves flowers. She'll be home tomorrow." Tony placed them in a tall vase, and took them to the dining room, to the center of a thick, hand-made, oak table.

The tall police officer unpacked his cooler where everything was kept warm, except for the salad he had topped with an ice pack. "My parents came to visit for a couple of months last year. I learned to cook Ethiopian foods from my mother. She was a renown cook in Bahir Dar, where she used to have a little hole-in-the-wall restaurant before she met my dad. She taught me how to make many traditional dishes while she was in the States." He continued. "Let's eat while the food is warm. I brought enough for Antonia, you'll have to warm up the dishes for her tomorrow."

After washing their hands, they sat down on either side of a large platter covered with half a dozen colorful mounds of foods. With pieces of spongy injera flatbread, they picked up small bites of spicy fava beans, buttery collard greens, curried yellow lentils, a dark red legume purée with a Berbere sauce, and a sweet and savory cabbage, potato and carrot dish with ginger and turmeric. They finished the meal with a tomato and cucumber salad that helped cool down their palates after the fiery fare. At the end of the meal, JR opened a small flask and poured two small glasses of a honey golden brew.

"Tej," he said. "It's a traditional fermented mead with gesho berries."

It was sweet and flowery with a slightly sour aftertaste. The berbere purée was Tony's favorite. "JR, what a wonderful meal! Thank you. You have created something fantastic with the spicy fava hummus. What is it called and what's your secret?"

With a smile, the tall man replied: "It's called Shiro Wat. But I cheated on my mother's recipe and americanized it, sweetened it, for our palate. I added smoked paprika and extra cardamom to the many spices in the Berbere mix. I used Indian holy basil, instead of the wild Ethiopian basil that I couldn't find. And at the last minute I blended some wildflower honey into it. Glad you liked it."

They spent the next hour talking about what service JR needed from them.

"I'm debating retiring as my wife wants me to do. I have more than twenty-five years in, and should get a fairly good pension as a major. But the Chief wants to appoint me as his deputy. That would mean more commitment, more work, and of course more money. But right now, I would prefer having some extra time for my family. In a few years, my kids will be done with their studies and living their own life. I'd like to spend more time with them before they move away. Although

I do get along very well with the chief, I do have a quandary, somewhat of a stain on my recent past that I would like to resolve before I make a final decision." He took a couple of long breaths before resuming.

"I need to find out what happened to John Daniels, one of my officers from Socorro, who committed suicide about three months ago. I could not get any clear answers from his family, his friends, or any of his co-workers. I went to see your friend Rosetta a couple of times in the last two months, but she was cryptic with her answers. She said that now that I have come to terms with my ancestry, I needed to look at how I am educating my officers. And last Friday, the second time I saw her, she told me that you two are indirectly connected to the same officer, although you are not yet aware of it. Then she mentioned that the answer lies with a woman's ghosts. That was all she could tell me. I don't know what to make of it."

More ghosts, Tone.

Although JR had a light skin pigmentation, a couple of years past he had confided to Antonio that his maternal ancestors were dark-skinned Africans. It seemed that he was now reconciled with his ethnic past. The Tonys were glad to hear that he had seen his parents the previous year.

"So JR, what would you like us to do?"

He took a deep breath and said: "Monday, I talked to John Daniels' wife, Linda. She lives in Socorro. I felt that she did not tell me all she knew about her husband. She is a little Latina, who seemed to hide a feisty temper. After her husband killed himself, she would hardly look at the investigator or at me. If this had not been filed as a suicide, I would have thought her a prime suspect. I'd like your sister to study her first, then maybe you could look at Daniels' friends. Would the two of you mind? Of course, I will pay your standard fees for this. I need to know what happened. At the very least, this should improve the training of my officers."

"JR, we've worked together before. We'll just charge you for our expenses. Send us what you can about this officer, his co-workers and his family. We'll look into it. And actually, we are currently doing some research for a missing person near Magdalena. We're planning on going there tomorrow. We can swing by Socorro on our way back."

"Can I help with your other search?"

Tony hesitated before asking: "Do you have access to Navajo records, mostly those of the Yellow Mud Bear clan."

"I'm sorry, but I don't have access to federal files. I'll send you what I have on Linda Daniels and the officer's co-workers. It's all confidential, of course."

On his way out, he shook hands with Antonio and added: "What is the name of that Indian man you're looking for?"

"Her name is Honaw Nez Begay, of the Yellow Mud Bear clan. Here, let me write it down. And thanks."

As he was walking back to his car, he turned around and said: "I don't know if I'll be able to access anything about her, but I have a friend who may."

~~~

José showed up a few minutes later. He was bringing news of Gisela and her brother Ray. He had gone in the morning to see Mrs. Mendoza, and take pictures of her mother's jewelry on his phone. "What a nice old-fashioned lady! She served me tea and cookies. She talked about the big Silver City fire in the mid 1800's, and how after the town was cleaned up, they built houses out of clay bricks, rather than wood. Then she said that her grand-parents told her that a few years after the fire, they witnessed the huge flood that carved the canyon right behind her place and how the back door became the front entrance to the house. She knows a lot of the local history."

After showing the pictures to various antique and pawn shops with no result, he had gone back to Cliff and Gila and had asked questions about the Alvarez clan to various persons he knew there. Three of those that responded thought that both Alvarez children were holed up at their father's place. They all alluded to Raul's violent temper. One of the neighbors' daughter thought that Gisela, or Jills as she was also known, was living in a trailer park in Deming, in an old tan and green mobile home. José said that he would go check on that soon. He also told them that he may be helping his friend Deputy Maria with a disturbing find in the Gila River, downstream from the Alvarez'. Being in the area would help him keep an eye on Raul's kids.

Mrs. Mendoza's banker would not release any information about when the checks were cashed, but the dear lady would receive her bank statement in a couple of days. She told him she would be glad to share it with him over a cup of tea. A smile lit up his face as he mentioned it.

The Tonys thanked him for his help. "You'll just have to

make another date with Mrs. Mendoza in a couple of days!" Antonio teased.

Antonia continued. "When you're not dating nice old-fash-ioned ladies, we would like you to research the history of a State Police officer — John Daniels, his wife Linda, and also his parents. The man was only thirty-one years old when he allegedly committed suicide, without a note or previous indi-cation that he would do so. JR is supposed to drop off some files on him."

Didn't need another case, but it's JR's.

Curious to find out what Rosetta thought? Indirectly connected to Daniels? Maybe we should go see her soon.

Let's! Before we go visit Claire.

~~~

Chapter 7

Rosetta Stones

Early the next morning, they left for Deming, just an hour away from Las Cruces, to visit their friend Rosetta. They did not have an appointment, as she rarely answered her old-fashioned, black, rotary phone, but knew that she was home most of the time, although they may have to wait for her to have time to see them.

Eight years back, when they first met Rosetta LaFLeur, she recounted how when she was in her late thirties, her principal client was the New Orleans Police Department. They kept her very busy as a clairvoyant advisor and she hardly had time for her private clients. One day NOPD asked for her help in discovering a potential serial killer. The man had actually been in her thoughts for the previous two years, nagging at the back of her mind constantly like a persistent hovering ghost, ever since he had started staging his horrible kills. By his fourth victim, she could hardly concentrate on her daily routine, the sentient presence so overwhelming. She knew then that he lived close to her in the French Quarter. One evening, she happened to see him at a liquor store, a couple of blocks away. His aura was so dark, no one in the store would venture near him. She could smell death pouring out of his very pores. He stared at her, as if she was someone he may have known. She felt fear exuding out of her body, and immediately left the store, as she knew he would feed on it if she came too close to him. Right away, she went to see the police lieutenant she had worked with earlier. With her description of the man, the officer hung out near the liquor store and was able to find the killer's whereabout shortly after. A year later, the day the man was finally incarcerated in a high-security prison, one of her friends who lived in Deming, asked for her help. She left that same day and the overwhelming feeling of doom faded, then disappeared, as soon as she had distanced herself a few hours from the 'Big Easy'.

~ ~ ~

At eight in the morning, Rosetta was home, finishing a breakfast of jellied toast and coffee with chicory. When they walked in, her attractive, sculpted face topped with lush, dark, crinkly hair offered them a most beautiful smile. Her tall cocoa-colored body was hiding under a generous purple and sky blue Mumu. Tillie made a beeline for her friend, a calico cat, who was curled on a padded shelf, purring, while staring at the dog. Rosetta offered the twins some coffee, the way they liked it, without milk, sugar or chicory. They first chatted about what was going on in their respective lives.

After giving her a large bag of dark-roasted Sumatran coffee beans, the Tonys approached the reasons they were there. "We have four cases going on at the same time. "

Rosetta was listening while shuffling a deck of cards.

Antonia started: "One involves a young helpmate who

stole jewelry and a dog from an older woman. Another one is about a missing Native woman, looking to help cattle and other factory farmed animals." Antonio took over in his deeper voice, as if worried his sister would get all the credit for the telling: "Another one is about a rancher who gets a bunch of calves stolen every year. And the final one is about the unexplained suicide of a young cop."

The Tonys looked expectantly at the seer and waited for her deductions. She spread her cards in a half circle, face down, and picked one from the pack. She turned it over and placed it on the left side of her table. The card showed two people facing each other, standing on a small island, one's skin is dark blue, the other is light green. Above a sky of stars, below a moon crescent peeking out of the earthen floor. Golden lightning on the left side, dark grey clouds on the right. Then Rosetta shook a small leather bag, and fished out a few crystalline rocks which she placed in a line to the right of the card. A pointy yellow one; a six-sided transparent purple crystal; a shiny, round, green pebble; and last a rough, white and black, granite stone. She looked at them for a couple of minutes, then shuffled her cards again. She cut the deck and chose the top card which she put to the right of the stones. This one showed a woman hanging by a vine around her feet, upside down, high near the top branches of a tree. Ravens and small red birds circled around her feet. Big black and red roots swelled out of the ground, reaching up to her upside-down head. After staring at her tools for a while longer, Rosetta closed her eyes and sat still and silent.

"The two of you will be caught in the middle of an inner lack of balance for a few days. Obstacles left and right will hamper you for the next week." She shuffled her cards and fanning them, offered them to the twins. "Pick one or two."

The card they chose showed four different multi-colored lizards, each facing the cardinal points, inside a circle made of stones, sticks and bones. A spiral above them started as dots at its center but changed to stars.

Antonio blurted: "This card looks different from the ones you showed us before."

Rosetta answered: "Yes, this one and the first one, the two people standing on an island, were painted by Mora. I think she had the two of you in mind when she created that one. She has added a few more to my collection. She is definitely connected to my long-gone ancestor and is being guided by her. She even paints like my dear mentor. Use her, as she is developing her potential and her new skills."

She paused and after staring at the card, continued in a softer tone: "The little dog is fine, and will be found soon. I see four men in the cases you are investigating, involved in very negative ways to damage others and their possessions. One of the four connivers is no longer a part of this team. Another one has mixed feelings about his surroundings and is changing his ways. The other two are absolute scumbags."

She had them pick up another card. This one showed a bear and a lion facing each other. Above the two animals were dark clouds scattered over blue sky, below them red flames danced on dark blue water.

"A little bear, a big she-bear and a big man-bear will connect spiritually and move toward getting together in the near future." She paused and began brewing herself another cup of chicory coffee.

The Tonys knew that this would be all they would get from Rosetta that morning and left her, calling for Tillie who had been laying down on the floor, the still-purring calico cat between her front legs.

What's with more bears? That was mysterious as usual.

Yes, Tone, but you know she only tells us what she sees, and it proves to be right every time. It looks like we need to follow up with Mora and Angel.

Wonder how dangerous is the very negative ways of the four men?

Dangerous enough she mentioned it. The cases may be connected.

That would be quite a coincidence, Sis!

No, just an intricate way for us to find out what we're looking for. On the positive side, the poodle will be found soon!

~ ~ ~

On their way to Magdalena, José called them. "I found out quite a bit on John and Linda Daniels. Much of it on the internet, some from old colleagues and the rest from files just dropped off at the office by a State Police officer. The forensic doctor who did the autopsy on John, said that she found traces of someone else's blood under one of his fingernails, and gunpowder on his right hand. He was right-handed. Forensic could not find a DNA match to the A positive blood found on John Daniels' fingers. I also discovered that he was the fourth of six siblings. His father was a cop as well. He was supposed to be really tough on crime and tougher on his children. He

75

died in a shoot-out when John was eight years old. According to the detective in charge of looking into Daniels' death, his wife Linda would not cooperate during the first interrogation. She later mentioned she wanted a divorce, and was afraid that it led him to end his life. She was a main suspect in her husband's death, but the gunpowder on his right hand exonerated her. She had a twin brother, an alcoholic, who committed suicide five years ago. Their parents were alcoholics. They died in a car crash last year. Linda has recently applied for jobs in Socorro and Belen. I can look some more on her, if you need. Later today, I'm going to Deming to look for a tan and green mobile home. I'll call you if I find anything."

"Thank you so much, José. We think we have enough on the Daniels, for now. We'll see what else we can find in Socorro. We're on our way there now and then off to Magdalena. Then we'll go up to see Claire in Santa Fe and be back tomorrow. Be careful in Deming. If Gisela's brother is with her, he might be violent like his father. And go see Rosetta, while you're in Deming. We're sure she'd be glad to see you."

A few minutes later, their cell phone rang again. Their girlfriend Claire first apologized, then told them that she had to fly to Houston that evening and may not be back for a few days. The twins were very disappointed as they had not seen her for almost a month and were looking forward to spend some time with her.

Wish she would tell us what she's working on.

She can't do that, Tone. She'd be fired from her agency if she did. Integrity is as important to her as it is to us. We can have sushi with a couple of friends when we get back.

No, Sis. Am just bummed about not seeing her. Should we abort and start again day after tomorrow?

We're half way there. Let's just go to Socorro first, see what we can find out.

Do you always have to be so bossy?

My half of our brain was born first!

Antonio mentally sent her Rosetta's picture of a lion and a bear under black clouds, their feet above fire.

~ ~ ~

Chapter 8

Friends or Foes

Tₕₑy had no firm plans for trying to get information from Linda Daniels besides using the twin brother's angle, so they just drove to her residence after deciding that Antonia would be the one trying to connect with her.

Mrs. Daniels lived on the East side of town, not too far from the Rio Grande. They parked a couple of houses down from a pretty little one-story building, with a flowering rose garden. As Antonia put a leash on Tillie, the front door opened and Mrs. Daniels walked out with a small black and white terrier on a lead. The dog barked at Tillie, before its owner called it back. She then waved at Antonia and moved toward her. "Don't mind him. He is just a bluffer, protecting me."

Perfect intro, Sis.

Antonia seized the opportunity. "Hi, he doesn't look too threatening. Thanks for letting me know. Would you know of a good place to walk my dog?"

"Hi, my name is Linda. Is that an Australian shepherd? He or she is beautiful."

"Thanks, Tillie is a girl Aussie, and she's been cooped up for an hour in the car. She needs a place to run. I was told there is a small park nearby."

"That's where I'm going. Looks like Jiminy and Tillie will get along." She replied after watching the two dogs sniffing each other.

"Wonderful! My name is Antonia, or Tony. I do appreciate your help."

They walked in unison, both dogs leading the way.

Soon they reached the bank of the Rio Grande. It was low. The local farmers and those upstream were watering their fields as it had been a very dry month. The farmers downstream would be lucky to get any water from the shallow river.

They turned the dogs loose, both of them running to the slow ribbon of water between the broad sandy edges. The two women sat on an old cottonwood log.

Antonia started. "I've been looking at various places in town. Can you tell me what kind of entertainment Socorro has to offer?"

Linda laughed. "Unless you like to go to bars, not too much happens around here. It's a farming and ranching community, and then we have the university and its assortment of students. The Capitol bar has live music once a week. Mainly local yokels. Nothing too exciting. And the theater is at least two months behind on the latest movies. You want entertainment, you have to go to Los Lunas or to Albuquerque."

Antonia kept her talking for a while, then asked her about shopping and local markets. Shortly after, Linda told her she needed to go to Brooks supermarket for a few things, and would she want to go with her?

They left the dogs in Linda's back yard, where they started playing run around in circle, then drove to the supermarket in Tony's pick-up.

Dual Issues

Linda made a beeline for the liquor aisles on one side of the store, and gazed at white wines, yet she did not seem ready to purchase any. Antonia put a couple of bottles of Cabernet Sauvignon in her carriage, before asking the other woman: "Thank you so much for your help today. Can I buy you a bottle of Chardonnay?"

The woman stared vacantly at her before talking. "Do you have anyone in your family who drinks himself under the table?

Opportunity knocks again, Sis.

Tony quickly answered: "I have a twin brother who can drink till he almost falls over. But myself, I only like an occasional glass of dry, smooth red. How about you?"

Thanks, Sis. Didn't mean for you to degrade me! Thought you liked to drink too!

Linda replied: "You have a twin brother! So do I. Or did, until he drove drunk into a cement pier holding a bridge. My mom and dad were alcoholics. I haven't had a drink since my husband passed away. He drank too. I go to my AA meetings three times a week. I've got one later today. Would you come with me?... Please?"

"I'm sorry. When did your husband pass away, if I can ask?"

With tears in her eyes, Linda replied: "Three and a half months ago." After she had wiped her eyes, both women made a few more purchases and moved to the store's register. Antonia asked her where the meeting was. Linda invited her to come to her place for half an hour, then they could go together to the meeting.

~ ~ ~

The AA meeting was held at the back of the community center, in a large room, barren but for a dozen chairs in a circle, already occupied by a few people. By the door, a small table with coffee and cookies. A burly man, with a generous, dark mustache, greeted Linda with a big hug, then shook Antonia's hand with a genuine smile. "Welcome. I'm Jorge. Everyone is welcome here, and a friend of Linda is my friend, too." It was probably a rehashed line, but the exuded warmth coming from the burly man made her feel comfortable to be there.

As soon as the director sat down, a few motorcycles were heard pulling over right outside the slightly opened windows. The bikers came in through the back door, all three sporting beards and pony tails, wearing blue jean jackets cut-off at the shoulder displaying their colors: "Riders of the Sun". A grinning skull donning dark goggles and flying golden hair was embroidered on the vests' back. Noisily, they sat down as Jorge welcomed them.

Tattoos covering both arms all the way to his shoulders, a short and thin biker started: "Five days, man! That's the best I can do. Saturday was a real bummer. My babe left me. My truck broke down. And I did not even mention my dog. Do I sound like a country song?" He added with a grin.

When it came to Linda's turn, she simply said: "Three months, fourteen days, and still sober. Nothing's easy." After everyone had applauded her, she turned to Antonia.

"Hi everyone, my name is Tony. I drink in moderation, but my brother does not. I will try to bring him in to a meeting." Linda was beaming at her side.

Dual Issues

Like hell you will, Sis! Want us to get tattoos and ride a tweaked Harley?

After the meeting, Antonia invited her to the pizza parlor in town. They both talked about not having any children. Tony said that she was so busy that she would not have time for kids. She also let her know that she did not think she could conceive. Linda opened up. "Another thing we have in common. I can't have kids. I've miscarried eight times, each time two or three months after... You know." She shook her head sideways and raised her shoulders.

Tony replied: "Oh no. I'm so sorry. The doctors could not help?"

Linda had tears in her eyes. She looked angry. She spoke loudly. "He killed them. He killed them, one after the other." People turned around at the sound of her voice. Antonia put her hand on her wrist. That seemed to calm her down a little.

In a softer tone, Linda sobbed: "It was John. My husband. He would drink, then he would kick me in the stomach, cause I would not... You know."

Shaking her head again, she whispered. "I would not have sex with him, cause I did not want to lose the baby. So he would drink, and get mad, and kick me, and kick me. And then I would lose the baby. And then I would drink till I passed out. And then, a few months later, it would happen all over again."

She looked around, but the other patrons had gone back to their meal. She seemed ashamed of her outbreak. Antonia tried: "This must have been so hard for you."

Whispering again, the woman said: "It was my fault that he committed suicide. I should have let him do what he wanted, since I was gonna lose the babies anyhow."

"Linda, it was not your fault. You did what you thought was best for the babies. And getting kicked in the stomach was certainly a sure way to lose them. Alcoholism is a sickness, as you know. There may have been something else that drove him to do that, but it definitely wasn't your fault."

Tears started rolling down the woman's face again. "He was a cop. And his dad was a cop too. That's a really hard job! He would get angry when something bad would happen at work. And he was doing extra shifts, so we could take a vacation. And then he said he would stop drinking and we could try to have a baby... But maybe you're right. Maybe there was something else... You know. He used to..." She stopped.

She quickly swallowed a sip of coffee. "On some of his days off, he used to hang out with these two friends from high school. I didn't like them. They were kinda obnoxious. And when they got together, they would get really shit-faced, you know. Pardon my French. Anyway, the last time he was with them, he came home with blood on his clothes. And when I asked him what happened, he got mad. And he said it was none of my business. But the next morning, it was a Monday, and just before he left, he said that he and his friends had almost killed an innocent bystander. And then he got in his patrol car to go to work, and then he killed himself right after he turned the corner." The tears were flowing again.

Antonia could not help but ask: "Would you like to find out what really happened? Maybe I can help? Find his friends? Did his friends come to the funeral?"

Linda looked angry and snapped. "No! They didn't even send flowers or anything. Some friends they were, right! And I don't ever wanna see them again."

Tony thought that she would have to find a different way to get in touch with the 'friends'. She took Linda home. Tillie was glad to see her.

He must be Rosetta's ghost, Sis.

Need to find out who he went to high school with.

Right. Don't think we can get anything else out of her. She might get suspicious.

Don't know. She was spilling those French beans pretty easily.

Tired, let's find a place to spend the night.

Sushi?

Yes, but not forgetting that you called me a drunk!

Just part of the job, Tone.

~ ~ ~

Chapter 9
Many Ghosts

IN THE MOTEL THAT EVENING, THEY WATCHED THE news and found out that a Mrs. Diane Hunter of Las Cruces, had been strangled by her husband with a necklace of pearls. The man had restrung the pearls on a copper wire, placed the necklace around her neck and twisted it with a fork until his wife had fallen down dead. He had waited for the police and crying, had told them he still loved her.

Same woman who called us, right?

Yes, but she did not hire us. Could not help her without her consent.

Thought you were psychic, Miss know-it-all!

Am not Rosetta. Know that! Feeling bad enough like it is.

Will drink to that, cause am the zonked-out one in the equation!

~ ~ ~

After spending an uncomfortable night in Socorro, the twins left early the next morning for Magdalena, the last place Honaw was seen. The breakfast of sushi leftover still tasted good, but they had drunk the whole bottle of saké the night before and woke up with a couple of headaches. They missed their friend Claire. Antonio was in a horrible mood and kept asking his sister to go home and forget about the assignment with JR. Antonia would not have any of it.

We're here and we're going to finish this job, now. So get it together!

Yes, Boss! But want to stop caring for others, get drunk and pass out. Just leave me alone!

That would be nice to do once in a while, Tone. Without your wanting more all the time, wouldn't drink as much.

You're perfect, Missy! Am the evil one.

Quit being a jerk! We'll see Claire next week.

Just a half mile from the little town, an odd sculpture caught their eyes. A twisted bicycle hung up vertically onto a tall metal pole, its wheels bent at an impossible angle, its chain holding an old leather wallet, the whole mess painted like a rainbow. A pair of mismatched cowboy boots that had been spray-painted hot pink, dangled near the bottom, while a dime-store crown of glittery red, white and blue feathers topped the contraption. Completing the absurd work, neon plastic flowers, assorted stuffed toys, a child's green bow with red arrows studded the display. A small brass plaque at the bottom claimed: The Big Indian Woman, by Jeremy Jones.

Think we found where it happened, Sis, and this is not a work of art.

Antonio was holding the car keys that morning.

The name on the mailbox of the third house from the horrendous sculpture read: J. Jones. Their job just got easier. They stopped. Antonio jumped out and holding his cowboy hat in his hand, he rang the bell.

"Coming," said a voice from behind the house. A tall man in his thirties, wearing a welding mask above his forehead, approached Tony. Tillie barked once, her hackles raised.

Even Tillie doesn't care for the artist, Sis.

The man removed one of his welding gloves as he reached Tony. "Jeremy Jones. How can I help you?"

Shaking the proffered hand, Antonio replied: "Hi, Tony Urbani. Detective. You're the sculptor of that piece down the road, the Big Indian..." Jeremy interrupted: "Woman. Yeah! Nice hey?"

Don't answer that, Tone!

Can I puke on his steel toes?

Antonio could not help himself: "Different! Plastic! What does it mean?"

"It don't mean anything. I just built it around the bicycle that got run over, right there, in front of me. I saw the whole thing. I wanted to immortalize it."

Tony waited.

Jones continued: "I heard this commotion and then I saw Tippy, my neighbor, run out. One guy had run over this big woman's bicycle, kind of folded it in half. The woman was an Indian, I mean one of them Native, like they wanna be called. She had jumped off her bike before the pickup hit her and rolled off into the ditch. But then, when she got back on the road, he said she looked mad, like she was gonna tear into that driver. Tippy said that two other guys got out of the truck, and they started beating her up. When I got there, I saw her fight back. She was big, like a big man, but she didn't know how to punch. She grabbed one of them by the middle and squeezed him, till he was crying. But then the others kicked her and hit her in the face, until she let go of the short Mexican. Now me, I don't care for them Natives, but you don't hit a woman, and never in the face, even if they're ugly. That's what they kept saying. You're too ugly. Nobody wants an ugly Indian woman. Then they tossed her in the ditch. By that time there were four of us from Magda, so I think that's why they stopped hitting her and left. But she cursed them good!"

"What do you mean she cursed them?" Tony asked.

"She was really angry and like spitting blood. She told the short Mexican she had squeezed by the middle, that he was making too many ghosts and that he should stop or he would become one of them and be stuck among all the ghosts forever."

Now these are Rosetta's ghosts, Tone.

So, what does your highness deduct from this?

Those ghosts are related to Honaw, and maybe to Linda too.

What do we do with this bigot, then?

Ask more questions!

"So, Jeremy, did you get a plate number for these guys' car?"

"Nope. It was a big, white Ford truck. You're a detective! Are you working for that Native woman? What do you need to know?"

Without giving him time for reflection, Tony said: "Could I have a description of these three people?"

"Well, two of them were Mexican, like short and dark. But the driver was white, with black hair. Big. You should ask Tippy, he can tell you better than me."

With Jones in tow, they went to see Tippy next door. A gangly fifty year old man walked out of his home as they walked up

88

his driveway. "Hey, Jeremy. Whats going on?"

"Hey! This guy is a detective. Tony something. He wants to know about the three guys that beat up that big squaw."

"Tony Urbani. With Two Tonys Search Engine. Please to meet you.

Tippy straightened up and asked. "What can I do you for?"

"I'm looking into the accident that Honaw Nez Begay had here three months ago. Jeremy said you were there at that time."

"That's the big Indian woman? Yep. I saw the whole thing. I already told the cops. See, I was watering my fruit trees. These guys came from the hills." He tossed a thumb to the mountains behind him. "They were driving real fast and they ran over her bike, right there in front of me. She was fast. She jumped into the ditch a second before they hit her. They drove over her bike and they saw me, so they stopped. I don't think they would have stopped if I hadn't been there. Then that big woman came back up the road. Her hair was all messed up. Her clothes were dirty and torn up. She looked pissed. She was yelling at them. One of them got out of the truck with a stick, and talked back at her. He was gonna hit her. But she was fast and she grabbed him by the middle and was squeezing him so tight he couldn't breathe. So the other two got out of the truck and beat her up bad. In the face, in the belly, on her lower back. That's where it hurts the most, in the kidneys. So finally she got away from them. She screamed insults at them before they took off."

Jeremy cut in. "Yeah! She cursed them good!"

Tony asked Tippy "Did you have a chance to look at the vehicle license?"

89

"Nah! But it was a New Mexico plate for sure. Black with red and green chiles."

"Tippy, did you get a good look at these people?"

"Yes, sir! Two of them were Mexicans, one short, one medium, and the other one a tall Anglo. They were all wearing cowboy hats and cowboy boots. And they sure knew how to cuss, like my Mama would not want me to repeat. Then they went back to Socorro. But I haven't seen them here before."

Can we go home now, Sis?

Not until we ask Linda about ghosts!

Tell her what a drunk your brother is! Should mention that you have no problem drinking with me!

Enough already. John Daniels was short and looked Hispanic. Need to definitely look into what he was doing on that day.

~ ~ ~

The phone rang while they were on their way to see Linda Daniels. José said that he had some unusual findings he needed to share with them.

"Rosetta told me that it would be all right to mention it to you. Now, this may not be related to the Alvarez case but it could be. You know that I've been helping Maria, my deputy friend in Gila, with a gruesome discovery. She told me yesterday that about ten days ago, a human body part was located in the Gila River, just south and down stream from Ralo Alvarez's farm."

Antonia wanted to know how far from the farm and if the sheriff's department had started DNA testing.

"They found an arm about a mile from Alvarez. It was

caught in some weeds on the East bank, just above where Duck Creek runs into the Gila. Maria knows we are looking for Mrs Mendoza's young helper in that area. That is why she told me about it. The bone of that left arm was cut by a coarse saw. It looks like it was frozen for a long time before it was gnawed by coyotes and dumped in the river. The fingerprints are long gone. They tested the DNA but could not find a match. They think that it could have come from a Hispanic woman upriver. It would have happened well before Gisela disappeared, but the proximity of the find near the farm makes them wonder if anyone there could be involved in the crime."

Antonia wanted to know: "What else have they found? Have they dredged the river and searched its banks, above and below the find?"

He answered. "They did. Above, well into the wilderness and below, all the way to the edge of the Big Burro Forest. They think it may have been an accident. Someone looting one of the Indian ruins. It seems that the FBI is letting them search for a little while longer before they moved in. Please, don't mention it to anyone."

"Of course, we won't," answered Antonio.

José told them that he had talked to Rosetta without telling her the particulars, just calling it a find. She had said not to involve Mora and her friend Osito. That it would be too much to digest for the boy. She also thought that drugs were involved, and that we would not find any more pieces in the river because most of it had been disposed of already. "I'm always amazed how she knows so much." He continued. "I'm going to relay that info to Maria, but I won't mention Rosetta's or your help. Anything else I should mention?"

Antonio advised: "They should test the sample for drugs. They should also research how many freezers are owned above Duck Creek near the river."

José replied that they had checked that, but all the people living there would not talk to the sheriff without a warrant. "It's a very tight community. Most of them are related by family. The few that I know will talk to me but they won't talk to the cops."

~ ~ ~

It was close to noon by the time they arrived in Socorro. Linda was walking her dog, wearing a pink flouncing dress and thick high heels. Antonia put a leash on Tillie and approached her.

"Good morning, Linda. I'm still in town. I'm leaving this afternoon, but I should be back in a few days. What are you up to?"

"Oh, I've had John on my mind a lot lately. I was thinking about going to see Father Marshall and talk to him."

"Can I help? You want to talk about it?"

The two women and their dogs walked toward the river. When they removed the leashes, the dogs immediately ran around zig-zagging, sniffing everything in their paths.

After a while, Antonia thought she should breach the subject of ghosts. "You've been thinking about John and that got me remembering about my aunt Sandra, who died a few months ago. Just about the time your husband passed away."

What aunt is that, Sis. Another lie?

Working! Be quiet!

"My aunt used to believe in ghosts. She said she could see them in her house on some nights. Sometimes she would not go into her friends' house if she thought there was a presence, a ghost in there. Do you believe in ghosts, Linda?"

The petite woman took her time answering, staring at Tony, as if not sure of a proper answer. "I kind of believe in them. I think my babies are ghosts now. I think John is a ghost. Sometimes I can almost see him in our bedroom, before I fall asleep. You know, I can almost feel his breath on me. His whisky and beer breath. He believed in ghosts too. Actually, the night before he died, he said some woman told him he was going to be a ghost. Then right after that, he said how he was sorry for all my babies he had turned into ghosts."

She started blubbering, tears rolling down her cheeks. She wiped her nose with the back of her sleeve and continued. "I'm sorry but I can't talk right now. You're touching something that's too raw in me. I need to go see Father Marshall. I'll see you when you get back, OK?"

Suicide confirmed. Let's go home, Sis.

Let's. Am going to research John Daniels' school friends. Good to find out the connection between Daniels and Honaw!

Coincidence?

Connection! And there is some delicious spicy Ethiopian food in the fridge for tonight.

And your brother will get drunk on some cheap wine, tonight.

Sore player!

Liar!

~ ~ ~

Chapter 10
Joy Ride

With daniels' transcripts, the tonys found the high school's name, the year he graduated and a lot more that they did not need to know. It did not indicate who the officer's friends were. They researched the school newspapers but again did not find anything relevant. They needed to find whomever the Belen High School principal was at the time. They also read that Daniels had attended one year in Forest Law Enforcement at Western New Mexico University in Silver City. Antonia's friend Sunny Villegas had gone to WNMU before he went to UNM for criminal justice, where she had first met him. Maybe he still had contacts at that little university. She would talk to him in the morning.

~ ~ ~

At six on Saturday morning, José came over for breakfast. He was going to look at mobile homes in Deming. It could take him a few hours, as this town just off the interstate had a lot of trailer parks spread out through the city.

The Tonys had to leave right away for Antonio's appointment with Bill Laney. They were going to look at the Lower Animas pasture, where Bill had originally found drag marks and fence repairs a couple of years before. They had agreed that they would not communicate internally while in the young rancher's company. Antonio was still upset about being called a drunk.

On the ride to Hillsboro, Antonia reached Sunny as he was leaving for work. He told her he still had contacts at WNMU and always meticulous, asked for a lot of information about John Daniels. He also let her know that he had moved to Deming. He had transferred from the Doña Ana to the Luna County Sheriff Department and moved into his parent's home. They were both slowing down fast. His mother was getting forgetful and his father needed help with the farm. Sunny thought that not much would happen during the weekend but would get back to her as soon as he knew anything.

~ ~ ~

Tony was dressed down from when he first met the Laneys. Blue jeans, T shirt under a canvas jacket and a worn cowboy hat. Tall leather hiking shoes rather than cowboy boots. They met across the road from the ranch gate to the headquarters. Bill Laney was waiting in a new Honda side-by side. Tony locked his pickup truck and got in the all-terrain vehicle. They sped through the little town of Hillsboro and finally stopped next to a large gate on the South side of the pavement. No name on it, just a big No Trespassing sign.

The two track dirt road dropped down into a large valley. Bill was driving very fast to impress Antonio with his new toy. As soon as they were out of sight of the gate, Bill started talking.

He recounted how he had found tracks near a small state road, where they were headed. The fence had been cut and poorly repaired. "Definitely not a job done by a professional rancher! Five calves disappeared on that day. My brother had to come by to check on the fence. He would not take my word for it!"

Tony wanted to find out more about the siblings' relationship. "Maybe he just wanted to see it for himself?"

Bill went on a long tirade about how both his brother and father did not trust him, how his father only gave him menial jobs. They treated him like an irresponsible child. And only his mother understood him.

Antonio asked. "Do you feel that sometimes your sister is watching you? Mine is always correcting me, criticizing me like I'm some little kid, even though we're the same age."

"Right! Mine does too, pretty often actually. I'm the youngest, so she tells me what I should do. And my brother bosses me around all the time. He likes to dictate everything I do at the ranch." Then he talked about how when his parents did not need him, he would hang out with his old buddies, drink beer and chase girls.

They stopped to drop off salt blocks on a barren spot next to a watering hole where a dozen cows gawked at them, then they traveled on a two track trail parallel to the fence. A sandy road laid on the other side. Bill slowed down and pointed to a spot between two T posts as the place where he had located where the thieves had cut the barbed wire.

At the end of that dirt road on the other side of the fence, rested an old aluminum Airstream trailer. Tall weeds surrounded it but for a path to its front door. Bill asked Antonio point blank. "So, you like to chase girls or are you one of those puff jobs?"

"Hey, I don't think my girlfriend would like what you just said." Tony quickly replied.

Looking slightly contrite, Bill said. "Just one girlfriend! Sorry, man. When I first met you, I thought you were a fag. You were so dressed up! Like maybe you played both sides. A lot of guys are like that now."

Time to change the subject, Tony thought. "I wanted to look good for the job. Most of the time I work with town people. I have to look professional. What about you? Maybe you play both sides yourself." Then pointing at the old trailer, he asked. "Who lives here?"

Bill abruptly stopped the vehicle and jumped out. Tony had barely gotten out when the red-haired man tackled him. Antonio quickly ducked down out of the hug, then rising up he slammed his right fist into the big man's chin, followed by a left-hand jab into the middle of his chest. Bill let out a deep sigh, backed up a couple of steps, and laughing he bent down and rushed again at Antonio like a football lineman. This time, Tony's right fist aimed for the tall man's ribs, then he spun around and kicked the right knee with his left heel.

Bill went down, raising dirt as he fell. "OK! You're no pansy. You got my bad knee." He was panting hard. "You pack a mean kick, man. You're going to have to drive this beast. I don't think I can."

Tony was sorry. He told him he had acted on instinct, did not mean to hurt him. Bill was still smiling as he limped to the passenger side. "No problem. My fault. I had an old injury from when I played football for WNMU. I did not expect you to know martial arts... So anyhow, we sold this small piece of land to a buddy of mine. His uncle put up a trailer on a flat spot. He never lived in it. He died before he could use it. My buddy comes out and uses it for babes now and then, when he wants to keep quiet about it."

Antonio drove the ATV much slower than Bill. They arrived at the far corner of the pasture. A two-track trail going north looked like it hadn't been used for a while. Tony had noticed that Bill would wince whenever they hit a bump on the road. Since no other cattle theft had happened from that pasture, it was time to turn around. He still wanted to know the name and contacts of the buddy that had bought the place next to the southern end of the pasture.

Bill defended his friend at first. "He's a good guy. He helped us about five years ago, when we needed an extra hand and the Parras were too busy. He and his dad have a small ranch south of Deming. He would not do us wrong. No way!" He seemed to ruminate about it for a while. "Come to think of it, he did ask a lot of questions about when we work cattle. I reckoned he wanted to help with the round-ups. But then, he was always busy with something else when we could have used him. Now, you got me suspicious about everyone. Let me think about it a little bit."

Tony answered. "Bill, you hired me to find out about the thefts. Let me do it. He may be more willing to open up to a stranger than to you, since you two are friends."

"He is my friend. I've known him since we were thirteen. We played football together at Winnie Moo. But I can't believe he would do us wrong."

"Winnie Moo? Where is that?"

With a laugh, Bill replied. "That's just what we call WNMU."

Tony pried again gently for the friend's name and number. "He may have just mentioned to someone else when and where you were working your cattle. Let me know who he is and I won't mention where I got his name. I'll keep you posted on what I find."

"OK, Randy Landing, out of Columbus, right by the Mexican border. Do let me know what you find out. Now, can we go home. I want to take care of my knee. Turn left here. It's faster that way and you can drop off the last two salt blocks by the windmill on the way."

Tony still felt terrible for creating this injury, although Bill had asked for it when he attacked him. "Do you want me to take you to a doctor?"

"No! I'll just use horse liniment on it. Heats it up and takes the pain away." Bill replied sheepishly.

When they reached the first gate, Bill gave him the combination to the padlock. "We use the same numbers for all our gates. I'll tell father I told you, but I'm sure he won't mind, since you're working for us."

At the ranch house, Tony helped Bill limp to the door. His mother came out running. "William, did you hurt your knee again? I'll get the liniment." Not waiting for an answer, she turned to Antonio. "Thank you for bringing him home. Can I get you anything? Come on in."

Since it was still early in the day, Antonio decided to take a look at the other pastures on the northern side of the ranch. He had left the topo maps of the ranch in his pickup. Bill told him he would draw the roads and gates on them and Mrs. Laney insisted on fixing him a couple of burritos for lunch while he went to fetch the maps.

~ ~ ~

It took the Tonys a couple of hours to drive around the large ranch. The twins stayed near the fences whenever they could. At times, they had to walk some distance to inspect places where the barbed wires seemed altered. They found the spot Bill had marked on the map as the last place where calves went missing. Extra posts, many stays and new looking wire had been added to the fence. A dirt road paralleled that part of the fence on the other side, for a few hundred yards.

That must be the place. They reinforced it after the theft.

Could be that Winnie Moo buddy, Tone. Bill sure has a bad case of verbal diarrhea.

Come on, Sis! He likes to talk but he's not so bad. Did not mean to hurt him. Acted on instinct.

Know you did. We friends again?

Antonio responded by sending her again the mental image of a bear and a lion facing each other.

They had a few game cameras left over from a previous job and decided to put them on the edge of the pastures that had outside roads adjacent to them. They would research the best places to do this, such as those that were on the edge of

BLM lands or Forest leases. They were not going to mention their placements to anyone, even the Laneys, especially not to Bill, so the cat would not be let out of the bag by anyone inadvertently.

When done, they dropped off the ATV at the gate, as Bill had asked. As they were driving home, Antonia called José. "We should be back in an hour. We got quite a bit accomplished at the Walking 4. How are you faring so far?"

"I am still in Deming. There are hundreds of mobile homes in Deming. I have found three that match the description and have dogs inside that I could hear. In the first one, a woman with many children answered. She had never heard of Jills or Gisela. The second one has a dog with a big bark. It is still a possibility, but the third home has what sounds like a small dog. I called out the name Elsie and the dog was quiet for a minute. Then it whimpered before resuming its high pitch bark. One of the immediate neighbors said that a young couple lives in there and that their little dog yaps for hours while they are gone. The couple yell at each other a lot and never leave the house together. He is gone most of the time. She walks the small black dog in the morning and leaves the house before eleven. Then she is back in the evening. I believe I may have found Elsie. I have spent the last hour watching the trailer and waiting for someone to show up."

Antonia responded. "Be careful, José. Remember that her father is violent and the boyfriend is unknown quantity. Please, come home now. We can go look for Gisela and Elsie tomorrow early."

~ ~ ~

Chapter 11
A Black Dog

ON SUNDAY MORNING, AFTER A BREAKFAST OF wild mushroom omelet, toasted baguette slices slathered with soft goat cheese and a couple of cups of black coffee, José and the Tonys hatched a plan of attack for Elsie's recovery. The day before, the older man had left Deming and gone home after waiting until dark by the mobile home. No one had gone in or out of the house. Although they were not certain that their subject and the stolen dog lived in that trailer, Antonia felt that it was the correct place and thought she should be the one approaching Gisela. She would appear the least threatening to the young woman. José would wait in the car in case of trouble.

Since they had a couple of hours available before leaving for Deming, they had time to do some research. While Tony looked again into reports of accidents in Magdalena, José investigated Bill's buddy: Brandon Landing. When he was working narcotics, a few years back, he had heard of a man named Roger Landing. The man was suspected of bringing in drugs from Mexico, but was never caught. His close proximity to the border and the uncommon last name for this area made José think that the son would not fall too far from the father in his lack of respect for others' property.

On the way to Deming, Antonio mentioned the game cameras and where he thought they should be put up. Just two of them for a start. One by the fence break Bill had shown him in the Lower Animas in Lake Valley, just a few yards from where the theft had occurred. The other one near the last theft on the Lower Kingston pasture. They would place another one later, near the fence next to the upcoming branding, if there was an outside road near it. José said he could go this afternoon, if everything went well with the dog, take GPS readings of the placement of the cameras and get back to them.

It was close to noon and getting hotter by the minute, when Gisela finally emerged from her home. The little dog perfectly fit its description.

"Gisela? Jills? My name is Antonia. Can I talk to you for a minute?"

The young woman turned around intent on going back inside, fumbled with her key, unable to open the door. "What do you want?" She yelled back nervously.

Antonia grabbed the key she had dropped and opened the door. "Jills, I'm a friend of Mrs. Mendoza. She just wants Elsie back. I don't think she'll even press charges about the jewelry if you talk to her."

Once Gisela had calmed down, she started crying softly. Waiting for her to stop her tears, Tony notice the young woman's face. An old shiner on her right eye, a bruise on her chin, small red splotches on her cheeks. She was very thin, her eyes were sunken, her skin ashen.

Fist fights and drugs, Sis. Let's get out of here before the hit man shows up!

103

Elsie seemed to have enough food in her bowl, but she was turning in circles as if she needed to relieve herself. Hiccuping, Gisela told her how sorry she was and how Mrs. Mendoza had been so nice to her, even if she was a friend of her grandma. She had not and could not sell the fancy gold necklace. She knew how much it meant to the old lady. She would give it back to her and apologize.

Antonia let her know that she would return the dog and the jewelry the next day. That way Gisela could take her time before going to Silver City to apologize. She jumped at the suggestion. Antonia left her a business card, if she wanted to talk or if she needed a ride back to Silver City.

Once outside, the dog relieved herself and started whining. Tony put Elsie in a little cage she had brought with her and gave José the gold necklace and a porcelain brooch. "For Mrs. Mendoza, when you are ready."

"I'll take these to her this afternoon! I think, she cannot wait to have her little dog back. She is so attached to it. And I will offer her my grand-niece's services. She is a good, honest girl who needs a steady job."

~ ~ ~

José mentioned how Brandon and Roger Landing lived just half an hour south of Deming. Antonia wanted to ask the Landings' neighbors about them if possible. José knew a couple of people in the little, almost Mexican, border town of Columbus. That afternoon, they decided to see if he would be able to get more information about them.

After Elsie had eaten some fancy wet dog food and drank some water, she was put back in her cage. She acted as if she understood that she was going home, curled up on her pad and fell asleep. They drove south toward the border.

Taking a small side street away from the main road, they stopped by a cement-block house painted light green with hot pink trim. A small overhang shaded a porch with a naive mural of red and yellow hibiscus flowers over dark green banana leaves. A table and a few chairs waited in the shade. An older man came out and talked with José for a minute, then he went back inside, closing the door behind him. He reappeared with two cans of beer, closed the front door and after putting his index finger in front of his lips, he invited José to sit down on one of the plastic armchairs. They talked quietly for about half an hour. Then they both got up, shook hands and the old man went back into his house.

As soon as they got back on the road, Antonia exclaimed: "Well, that was mysterious. What did you find out?"

"The Landings are feared around here. The father is the mayor and tells people what to do. When to water their garden, when to have a fiesta, even when to have a wedding! If they don't obey, he raises the town taxes. But he does not improve anything. They think all the tax money goes into his pocket." José answered. "Then the son is known to deal drugs, but is protected by a cousin of the county sheriff. I did find out that Brendon likes to hang out at the Sleeping Lizard motel, or the Sleazy as it's known. It's a bar, restaurant and motel on the eastern end of Deming. The bar is called the Trail's End and is renown locally as a place to find whores and drugs."

"Perfect! Antonio can go there tomorrow." Antonia replied.

What's this? You want me to buy drugs now?

No! Just mingle with whores! Got a plan. We'll set a trap for the bastard. Talk later.

What if he's innocent?

Think Bill is innocent, Brandon is not!

~ ~ ~

José called Mrs. Mendoza. He first mentioned how he was sorry to call so late and on a Sunday, then he told her how Antonia had found her dog and some of her jewelry, and would she want to have them back today or tomorrow morning. The older lady thanked him profusely and asked him to come by at once. She also asked him if he would want to share some chile con carne that she was preparing for her dinner.

When Antonia dropped him off at the office, wishing him good luck on his date, José grinned at her as he transferred Elsie to his car.

~ ~ ~

Chapter 12

Three Bears

On MONDAY, ANGEL AND MORA WERE ONLY going to be available after school, after three in the afternoon. Antonia called Max and Lenmana to let them know about the meeting time. Max told her that he liked that time best, so that he could finish cutting the antlers. Tony did not want to ask whose antlers he was cutting.

Having some time on their hands, they went to install two game cameras at the Walking 4 ranch. The cameras were hidden inside the ranch, near the fence, and near adjacent dirt roads.

That morning, José was busy introducing his niece to Mrs. Mendoza.

Around noon, Sunny called to let her know he had news about John Daniels. He did not work Tuesdays and Wednesdays right now and could come by the next day in the morning. Antonia thanked him. "And since you're working in Deming now, would you know anything about a Brendon Landing?"

"Do I? Just me and the whole department! The kid has been on our radar for the last six months. Bad news, that one. Wait till you see the pictures I'm bringing you. It will cost you though!" Sunny replied.

"Lunch, tomorrow?" She asked.

"You got it! But it may not be enough. You're going to owe me dinner when you see what I got for you!"

The kid?

Right, Tone. Anyone immature around thirty is a youngster after you turn forty.

~ ~ ~

When Tony arrived at the school, Max and Lenmana were already there. The blind woman was beaming, seated astride a dun horse that Sirena was slowly leading around the courtyard. Max walked toward Antonia. "Your mother is amazing! She could tell Lena wanted to ride that horse. She had always loved horses, but on the Rez, we didn't trust any of them enough to let her ride one. And the horses I do get are either crippled or outlaws. This one is real gentle. You can tell by his face."

Sirena stopped the horse and helped the young woman come off her mount. Then everyone went inside the school.

Max handed Lenmana a package wrapped in brown paper, then he asked if he could stay for the session. Angel's mother agreed, as long as her conditions were met. The school nurse was the other person present that day.

Angel made his entrance on his tricycle, preceded by Mora. He looked around the room and got off his trike, then he wobbled over to Antonia and fiercely hugged her leg. He turned around and went to look at Max, who was sitting by Lenmana. The boy stood still, staring at the big man's face. As Max put out his hand to shake his, Angel planted his fingers on the man's knees and wiggled them. Mora asked: "Angel wants to know if you play the piano, Max?" The big man acquiesced, silently shaking his head a few times. Mora continued. "Angel would like to play the piano with you when we're done here, if that's all right?"

Lenmana handed Angel a package. "For you, for helping me find my mother." He tore open the brown wrapper, dropped the gift on his trike and shook his hands when he saw what was inside. A black velour pillow will an appliqué of light brown fur in the shape of a bear, with colorful beads stitched all around it. On the flip side, she had woven a golden owl. Both large eyes were made with slices of antlers. Its belly was laced with grey and yellow strings. "This is a good owl, an owl who knows the future." She turned her head toward Mrs. Torres to explain. "I tied strings rather than feathers so Master Angel would not swallow them." Angel licked the velour cloth on the edge of the pillow, then sat down on it.

Mora told everyone how they had worked with his electronic pad and her game cards. They were able to come up with a few new details. The ghosts are real people, not cartoon fiction, but they are no longer alive. They live in the shadow of others. There are three bad dog-people involved: one is a black wolf, the leader of the pack, one is a yellow dog, and one is dead, a ghost." She took a deep breath. "Osito is afraid of the black wolf. He thinks he is going to shake him, hit him and run him over. He doesn't want to talk about him any more." Angel had his head down and seemed far away. As his mother was asking him if he was all right, he perked up and shook his right hand at Max.

Mora continued. "He told me that a man-bear who plays the piano can find the woman-bear." She paused. "Is that you, Max?"

The big man suddenly got up and moved toward Angel. "I've been called a bear before. Thank you, Osito. You are a true wonder. How can we find Mama Bear?

At first, intimated by the big man towering over him, Angel backed up and fell over his tricycle. He got right back up before his mother could reach him, turned around and hugged Max's thigh. Then he straddled his tricycle and pointed to a piano on his laptop. He also pointed to cows, to beans, to a road, to a nose and then to a toilet, before going back to the piano.

Mora told everyone that they needed to move to the music room just next door. Strings and wind instruments lined up the walls. A beautiful grand piano occupied a good portion of the room. Max opened the lid and reached for the keys. He played a short blues line, as Angel came up and with Mora's help sat next to the big man. Carefully, he tapped a few notes. Max just looked at him, not knowing what to do next.

Mora told him: "Osito cannot sustain his calm composure for very long. Except on occasion, he can only play a few notes at a time, before he gets overwhelmed and jittery."

The child played again the same few notes.

"Wait!" exclaimed Max. "I know that tune. My dad used to sing it. He made it up. We all sang it when we were on the road. It seemed that we were always on the road when I was a kid." He was playing a simple little ditty. Angel seemed ecstatic, shaking his hands above his head and smiling.

Suddenly, in a deep baritone voice, Max was singing. "One more mile to go, we're going around the bend, one more mile to go, where will it ever end. Two more miles to go ..., and so on."

Mora asked: "Where were you going when you sang that song?"

"We lived in California. We were always going east."

"What did you do on these trips?" she asked again.

"We would do field trips, gather plants for my mom. She would make salves and tinctures."

"What did you do on your last trip east with your family?" She kept prodding.

"Right before she died, we gathered mesquite beans. Mom would dry them and grind them and add that to the flour of the cookies she baked. That was our favorite treat." He stopped. There were tears in his eyes. He turned to Angel. "That's it, little man. Isn't it? Mama Bear is in Mesquite, visiting cows that are making the road stink. Right!"

Angel was sitting on the ground, his legs folded, spinning around, shaking his hands, laughing. That was his happy sitting dance. Mora was clapping her hands. Sirena went to get apple juice for everyone.

~ ~ ~

Lenmana and Max conferred head to head, for a few minutes. Angel looked worried, hugged his pillow and gave the velour a serious lick before flipping it over and tasting the buttons made of antlers. Antonia moved over to the couple.

Max spoke up. "Here is what we think: Lena will stay here with somebody and I will take Osito with me right now, to look in Mesquite at the milk CAFO there. We should find Honaw easily that way."

Mrs. Torres got up and loudly said: "Oh no, you will not! Angel is not going anywhere but home, church or school. I will not let you take him anywhere. Just be thankful for what my angel, with the help of God, has given you."

Max got up and took Janice Torres' hands in his. "I apologize, Mrs. Torres. Angel is so aware, I forgot about his condition. Of course I will not take him away from you. Actually, if we are correct, all I have to do is go to Mesquite and look for her by myself." He turned to Lenmana. "Lena, if I go tomorrow, would you mind staying at the house. I'll feed everyone early before I leave in the morning. It's only a dozen miles from here, a couple of hours from home. I should be back before dark with Mother Honaw."

Lenmana agreed. Mrs. Torres offered to come stay with her, while the school was in session. The blind woman was quick to reply, with irritation in her voice. "I do not need a baby-sitter. I have stayed by myself many times before. I cannot feed the outside animals, but a young man next door will help if Max takes too long!" In a softer voice, she added: "I am very thankful to you, to Master Angel, to Mora, to Antonia and to God for everyone's help."

Before they left, Angel indicated that he wanted Max to play the piano again. They went back to the music room. The boy played a few notes, a few more than previously. Max smiled as he knew that song right away, and belted the lines while hitting the keyboard. "It's a long way to Tipperary, it a long way to go... "

~ ~ ~

Chapter 13
Bad Boys

Antonio called Rick Laney Senior to update him on what they were doing. He let him know that they had checked the fences in all the pastures adjacent to any county or state roads. All accesses from the National Forest would be too hard to get to for a fast getaway without leaving signs. "We have talked to the cowboys and friends who have helped you. They all seem honest and reliable. Your son, William was very helpful in helping us with our search. " He let Rick Senior digest that for a minute before adding: "Will you be working calves any time soon?"

The rancher replied that it probably would not be for another month. "The bulls have done their jobs well last year. I did add one extra bull per herd. That seems to have fixed the problem of scattered birthing dates. There should only be a few late-born calves, this year."

Tony made up a couple of names on the spot. "Have you ever used any of the following cowboys: Johnny Montoya..., Emilio Cordova..., Brandon Landing?"

Who's concocting names, now!

Rick Laney took his time before answering. "I used to know a Jesus Montoya, but he would be in his nineties, if he's still around. Never heard of Emilio Cordova. And don't ever want to deal again with any Landings. That whole family is trouble. Some people should be wiped off the face of the earth, if you ask me."

"Could you please, share what happened and why you will not deal with them?"

Impatiently, Laney answered: "William used to hang out with the youngest son, Brendon, during his football years. I am fairly certain he tried to give my son drugs. That may be why he injured his knee. By the way, thank you for bringing him home after he fell and injured it again."

~ ~ ~

Sunny Villegas showed up just before noon. "Hola, Antonia. Don't want to be late for lunch!" He gave her a hug and they went to sit by the dinning room table.

Antonia pulled out the food Antonio had prepared the night before. Sunny's favorite: a Mediterranean fare. Hummus, Baba Ganoush, Falafel with a tahini dressing, spicy K-bobs, a yogurt and cucumber salad and a flaky pastry with a pistachio filling.

"OK! You win the prize. Or did Antonio fix this for me?"

Antonia jested: "You know he's the better cook. I can hardly boil water!"

"Woman, how can I marry you, unless your brother is part of the package."

"Sunny, you're impossible! Your wife even know you're here?"

He still doesn't know am the better half of the package, Sis.

Sunny pulled out a folder from his briefcase. "Wait till you

see this. Daniels and Landing. Two bad hombres in one scoop."
He placed a picture on the desk. "I had it enlarged. Told you,
you'd owe me dinner, too!"

Six young football players were portrayed, all wearing
padded shoulders and jerseys with the Mustang logo, the
WNMU mascot. "¡Mira! Look! These are the 'Baaad Moos'! I'm
not making this up. That's what everybody called them. That's
what they called themselves. Chicos Malos, Baaad Boys. There
is Daniels. That's Ray Alvarez, and Bill Laney, then Brandon
Landing. And these other two are dead: Danny Romero, he
committed suicide. And James Marconi. He died in a car crash.
Romero was driving. So what do you think? Can I deliver the
goods or what?"

Coincidence?

No Tone, just the universe connecting the dots for us!

Antonia thanked him. "Half of them are dead, two sui-
cides! They did not pick a very lucky name."

Sunny told her. "All these kids were from ranching fam-
ilies, Alvarez's parents were farmers. That kid and Landing
are just big trouble. Drugs, trafficking who knows what from
across the border, stealing from snowbirds traveling in their
big trailers. We just need to catch them red-handed."

Antonia replied. "I heard that Landing's father might be in
the sheriff's cousin's pocket. Have you heard anything about
that?"

Staring into her eyes, in a very quiet voice, he told her.
"Look, just between you and me, Internal Affairs has asked me
to check one of the deputies for that matter and other simi-
lar wrong-doings. That was another reason for my moving to
Deming. It wasn't for the wind and the dust. That's for sure!
So you know, it's not Sheriff Gonzalez. He's clean. I'm pretty

certain. I've known him a long time. But Garcia, the deputy, all of the sudden got a brand new car, and paid off his mortgage early. Not too bright, but that's who we catch first, the dumb ones flashing their loot!"

They talked about the Moos that were left. Ray Alvarez was following his crooked father's foot steps, and would probably end up dead or in jail soon. Brendon, his siblings and his dad were on all the local law agencies' radars, especially narcotics. Bill Laney seemed to be the only clean one. Sunny knew that Laney Senior was known to be very rigid. They talked about setting up a trap for Landing.

"Do it. I'll help, but I won't tell my sheriff. Sierra County will probably help. Can you get any other agencies involved?" He asked.

She answered. "I'll get JR and State Police involved. He's got an interest in it too... How about dinner on Sunday?"

"Claro. You got a deal. I'm done with work at two in the afternoon. Tell Tony he better cook that meal, or I'm not showing up."

Told you Bill was a good guy!

OK, Tone. Maybe not when he was a Moos?

~~~

Max called to announce that he had found Honaw the previous night. She was hanging out with Lenmana today, but she had a job at the milk factory and she was going to return to it on Monday, for a little while longer. "That was amazing! She worked as a sort of vet over there at first. She took care of a bunch of milk cows and got the owners to stop giving them the hormone trash they were giving them to make more milk.

The cows quit getting sick. Some had even died before she got there. So the cows are not giving as much milk, but the milk has no pus in it anymore. She's got them persuaded to switch over to an organic farm. They're moving their operation to a place near Hatch, reducing their operation, and they are going to grow their own feed over there. But it was time. The government is shutting down on supporting the medium-sized farmers. You only get moolah if your business is real big! Wow! That was quite a feat. But leave it to Honaw. She can do anything when she puts her mind to it. So thank you for helping Lenmana find her mother. We'll come visit and pay you this week-end."

~ ~ ~

Antonia called Linda Daniels. "Hi, Linda. How are you?"

After a while she dove in with the Baaad Moos. "I remember that you were wondering about John's high school friends. I found a picture with him with a few friends. Would you like to look at it?"

Linda was not in a good mood, anger showing in her voice. "No! I really don't want to have anything to do with these bastards! Are you coming back to Socorro any time soon?"

"Linda, I have a confession to make. I did not tell you all the reasons I was in Socorro last week... I'm a private investigator."

"So, you lied to me. You were just grilling me because of John?"

"No, Linda. I've been researching an accident that happened in Magdalena. An Indian woman was attacked there a few months ago. The people that saw the incident said that they recognized one of them as being a WNMU student. I did some research and recently found a picture of your husband with five other football players. Then I thought about what you told me. Would you mind looking at it, let me know if you recognize anyone there? That would help me tremendously."

Mrs. Daniels thought about it for a minute. Since she was in Las Cruces visiting a friend for a couple of days, she agreed to come to the office the next morning.

~~~

Time for me to go, Sis. As planned, will casually let Brandon Landing know that am working cattle with the Laneys. Hope he takes the bait!

If he is as crooked as we think he is, he will. And Tone, won't say a word while you work.

Hope not. Need to be myself more often.

Tony dressed up as a cowboy, but with used clothes, a stained hat and old riding boots, and drove in his pick-up to the Sleazy Café in Deming.

~~~

Chapter 14

The Bait

THE SLEEPING LIZARD WAS A DUMP. ON THE eastern end of Deming, with sounds and view of the interstate, it looked like it had seen better days. At four in the afternoon, the place was packed. Tony spotted Brendon and friends at the very end of the bar. He went to sit at the only place left open, three seats away from the seemingly already drunk subject of his investigation. The counter had not been cleaned for a while. Old and crusty stains here and there, but better than the floor. Besides the overwhelming smell of spilled beer, there were also faint odors of vomit and urine. This wasn't a bar he would recommend to anyone. He ordered a branded beer in a bottle.

Now and then, he would glance furtively at Landing. It worked. The man came over to him, followed by his friends. "Hey, you got a problem, dude?"

Staying cool and unfazed, Tony answered. "I know you. You played for Winnie Moo. Didn't you?" The two shady friends went back to their corner.

"Yeah, I did. You played?"

"No. Did not even make the cut for the basketball team."

"So what's up? Just passing through?"

Tony thought that it would be hard to keep a dialogue going with someone he could not feel any affinity. This man was repulsive.

Tone, you know too much about him. Don't let it affect your plan. Start talking about ranching!

"No. Just doing some ranch work here and there."

That peaked Brendon's interest. "Yeah! Who did you work for?"

Not too fast!

"I worked for ranchers in Gila, in the Burros and in Hillsboro too. You cowboy too?"

Brendon stuck his thumbs into his pockets, puffed up his chest and said: "I got a ranch by the border. Pretty good size. It keeps me busy."

"Good for you! Let me know if you need a hand. I'm always glad for the work. What do you raise?"

"Mixed breeds, you know. Buy them cheap, then sell them with a calf by their side. I can get a lot of money from the Mexicans for a good pair. Where did you work last?"

Bet you bought them real cheap!

Butt out, Sis.

"I've been working for the Laneys. We just finished branding some young calves. They raise some nice beeves."

Not too thick, now!

It's good bait, Sis.

Brendon sat on the stool that had just been vacated, next to Tony. "I worked for them a few years back. The old fart is not easy to please. He made me go over some of the places I had already covered."

"Was anything back there?" Tony asked.

121

Looking down at the dirty floor, the braggart answered."Well, I might have left a pair or two behind. Old man Laney must have heard them bawling. I wasted another hour chasing those cows and calves. I sure don't want to work for that guy anymore."

"Yes, he is not the easiest to work for or his son Junior either, but he pays well."

"So which pasture did you work?"

Here we go, Sis.

"We worked the Lower Animas a couple of days ago. We finished the Greenhorn Canyon three weeks ago. Man, that's rough country. Not like the low Animas. It took us five days in Greenhorn! I thought we'd never find them all. Some were even in the forest. So, next couple of days, we had to fix the fences. Packed posts on an old mule and fought the thorns."

Brandon could not help himself. "Yeah! They still got cattle in that Lower pasture?"

"They sure do. Probably a hundred heads or so. We branded close to ninety calves".

Brendon tried to change to subject. "His wife only fed us bean burritos after a hard day's work, like we're some kind of wet-backs!"

Tony was fed up with this ungrateful jerk. "We ate pretty well last week. Bill brought us a beef and bean stew that Mrs. Laney made. And some warm tortillas and cinnamon rolls for desert!"

"Bill didn't ride?"

"No, he hurt his knee again!" Tony needed to call Bill as soon as he was done with this swindler.

"Yeah, he's a pansy! His father should have forced him to

ride. Well, I'll see you around. What's your name?"

"Tony. And you?"

"Brendon. Later, Tony." He left to join his friends. Soon they were whispering, with their heads together. Antonio left the stinky Sleazy.

Good work, Tone.

On their way home, Antonio called Bill. "Hey Bill, should someone ask you if you worked the Lower Animas pasture, please say yes, and that it was a few days ago, but don't tell them anything more. And by the way, you were not able to ride at that time because of your bad knee."

"OK. Will do. Sounds like you got some suspects?"

"I'll tell you about it next week, if all goes well. But keep it to yourself, please."

~ ~ ~

Linda came over early the next morning. She was impressed by the office. She looked at the picture and pointed to Brandon and to Ray Alvarez. "That's the bastards that hung around with my John."

"And what about the other three men?" Antonia asked.

"Never seen them."

Antonia offered her a copy of the picture, but she turned it down. "I don't ever want to see these guys again."

~ ~ ~

Chapter 15

Tying Up Loose Ends

As soon as Linda had left, Max and Honaw showed up. Honaw was an impressive person. Tall, dark braids hanging on either side of a large face that radiated kindness. Big hands. Antonia thought the two of them were like two big bears, just like Rosetta had said. They paid and thanked her. They were on their way back to the milk factory as Max called it. Honaw was only going to work for another week or two, just long enough to help with the change at the dairy farm, then after a short time at Max's to help with his animals, she would go back to the Rez up north with Lenmana. She had a lot of work to do there, as soon as she got back.

"Has your head fully recovered from the blows you received a few months back?" Antonia asked.

"It has. Thank you. I only feel bad for the man who committed suicide. I hope I did not enable him to end his life. I feel that he may have taken me too seriously. I told him about his unborn ghost babies. He was not ready to hear this."

"Honaw, you have not done anything wrong. You only defended yourself. The man was damaged and would have ended his life another time. By the way, I'd like you to look at a picture and let me know if you recognize anyone, please."

The big Native woman looked at the print and pointed to

Daniels, Brandon and Ray Alvarez. "These three looked a little older, but they are the ones who attacked me and destroyed my bicycle. I forgive them. They are foolish men. The two that are still alive, must change their ways or they will encounter many more dangers in their life."

Does she sound like Rosetta?

A little. Maybe Rosetta has some Native blood in her.

She has native Central African blood in her!

~ ~ ~

Antonio called JR to confirm Officer Daniels' suicide. "And I may need State Police's help. I've set up a trap for someone who knew Daniels and injured the Native woman I asked you to look into."

"Tony, I asked my friend but he could not get anything on her, which is not unusual for someone on the Rez. Many of them are not in the system. But as for your trap, you let me know when and where. We'll be there. How many of us will you need?"

"I don't know yet the particulars, JR. Probably half a dozen cops, plus a helicopter and a drone."

"I can't do the helo without an official written demand, unless it's an emergency, but I can come and bring someone to work our big drone."

Tony was relieved that lawmen would be available. "Thanks, JR. I'll call you as soon as I know more."

~ ~ ~

Mora was just driving through the entrance gate when the school opened the next day. Antonia had gotten there earlier to ask her a couple of questions. "Rosetta said I should talk to you."

"Sure. I've got about fifteen minutes right now. Then, I'll need to find Angel."

Tony told her about Max finding Honaw in Mesquite, thanks to Angel-Osito, as they walked to the garden and sat on a wooden bench. Neatly spaced rows of mixed flowers, herbs and vegetables were creating a refreshing oasis. On one side, red raspberries stood up straight, on the opposite side, brambles of unruly blackberries, just starting to turn deep purple, were sprawled over the path. Overhead, covering the whole garden area, was shade cloth, protecting the plants from the intense sunshine. The sunflowers were so tall that their heads touched the shade.

Mora took a pack of cards from her pocket. "How can I help?"

Straight to the point, she was following her mentor's endowments with giant steps. Antonia replied. "I need to find a missing or hiding man. He was with the other two who beat up the she-bear."

Mora offered her the pack. "Pick a card."

Tony flipped the card over: a large yellow ball with arms and legs splayed out. One foot in a waterfall, the other foot stands on sharp rock cliffs, one hand is touching the moon, the other is reaching for the sun.

"All right, pick another card."

That one showed the back of a naked person climbing a mountain, but the head is wearing a mask adorned with feathers, and is turned around like an owl's. Snow capped mountains in the background, a blue moon above and the creature's feet in the ocean,

Looking into her eyes, the young seer told her: "This insane man is hiding in the dark, near water. He was injured emotionally when he was young. Insecure. A puppet to a few men who abuse his willingness to be integrated. When he is ready to come out into the sunlight, he will try to burn someone for revenge. This will happen soon... Also, your brother needs to find his own destiny. Give him more space. Now if you'll excuse me, I have to find Osito."

She has learned well from Rosetta. And she's right. Need more space from you!

~ ~ ~

The rest of the day was spent going over bills and receipts. Antonio took over the accounting.

Let me take care of it, Sis. Do better with numbers than you!

Words are my forte, numbers are yours. Giving it up to the sharper half!

~ ~ ~

As they were walking Tillie on the banks of the Rio Grande, Claire called. "Hey, you two. I'm back at home. Mission accomplished." She joked, as she was always mysterious about what her job was. They had worked out that she most likely worked as an FBI agent or for another three-letter federal agency. She continued. "Can we get together this week-end? I miss you both."

Antonio took over the phone. "We better see you this week-end. Your turn to come down. We may have our own mission near Hillsboro in the next few days. And unlike you, Ms. Secret Agent, we might share with you what's going on."

Claire did not take the barb. "Be safe. I'll see you soon. Can I bring anything?"

"Yes, pick up some bluefin tuna from the "Fresh n' Salty" in Albuquerque on your way here. I'll call them so they can have some shipped in for Saturday morning. I'll see what else they have coming in. I'm going to fix us sushi. This time, you can't disappear!"

"Sweetheart, you fix me sushi and I'll be forever yours! And maybe Antonia's too!"

"I heard that" Antonia replied laughing, as she hung up the phone.

The Tonys were pleased that the rest of the day was slow. It had been too busy lately. They took Tillie for another long walk, so the bird dog that she wasn't could herd ducks to the middle of the river.

~ ~ ~

Chapter 16
The Trap

THE NEXT DAY STARTED EARLY WITH A CLATTER OF multiple phone calls. Sunny was the first at ten past five in the morning. "I got an intel from a very reliable source, that the Landings are saddling up and getting ready to trailer somewhere. You may want to call your friends. I will catch the Landings going through town, if they are going north."

The call waiting was from José. "Good morning. The friend I met the other day in Columbus, just called me to say that his neighbors are loading up their big trailer with at least six horses. I think Antonio's trap may catch a big fish today."

Tony called JR, who had been staying in Las Cruces that weekend. He had the drone team ready. They will follow the trailer when it reaches Hillsboro or Nutt. Four more state troopers were also ready to travel should the perps go anywhere near the Lower Animas pasture.

Then Tony got in touch with the Sierra County Sheriff's department. At first they were not too enthusiastic about the whole thing, until Tony mentioned the reward money for catching whomever was stealing Rick Laney's calves.

"Well, Sir, why did you not say it was for the Laneys. We'll be there at eight. Right where County Road 402 takes off State 57, on the South end of their Animas pasture, right?"

It was all Tony could do, to stop them from moving in too early and alert the thieves about the whole operation. "Please, have your personnel wait on stand-by until I know the suspects whereabouts. If you get there too early, it may compromise the whole proceeding. There is also a possibility that they may be going somewhere else."

"Roger that! We'll wait to hear from you."

Should have been a general, Sis!

You are, Tone. Keep it up!

~ ~ ~

The Tonys decided to take their chance and left for Hillsboro. If the fish did not take the bait, then they would go see the Laneys and hatch another plan. If the fish did bite, then a spot just above Hillsboro would give them good cell phone coverage and a back door in case of a possible escape. Of course Tillie was coming along. She loved going for rides, acting the co-pilot, sitting in front, with her snout outside the window, inhaling all the country smells.

Thirty minutes later, Sunny reached Antonio on his cell. "Tony, I just talked with JR. My contact said six horses and four cowboys are loaded and moving north. I've just picked up the County's drone. And lo and behold, its batteries are fully loaded. I am waiting for them in an unmarked on the South side of town, at Florida and Gold. If they come through Deming, they'll have to pass by me."

Thirty more minutes passed very slowly. Tony was worried that the plan would not work, or that they did not take the bait.

It will work, Tone. Relax.

Relief flooded Antonio when he heard Sunny's voice. "They just pulled in at the fuel station, north of Deming. They went in the restaurant there. There are four of them. And get this, deputy Jerry Garcia and Ray Alvarez just drove in with a long empty trailer. They went into the restaurant and sat down with the Landings. They're having breakfast right now. How's that for surprising news?"

"Sunny, that is wonderful news. I was starting to doubt my plan. I'll call everybody as soon as you tell me they are turning on highway 26."

Sunny responded. "I've just tossed a couple of yellow fluorescent paint balls on top of the Garcia trailer. That should make it easier for the helicopter to spot them if they get off the pavement."

"There won't be a helicopter available from State, but the paint will make it easier for the drones. JR said that they will have a drone too. They have a big one, they can fly it a few hundred yards above yours. And Sunny, if Garcia is in on it, we'll need to keep in touch through cell phones. He probably has the county radio on him or in his truck." Tony replied.

"Good call on the radio comm, Tony. Let me call you back in a few. I may have access to more equipment and personnel."

Antonio called JR and told him that all communications would be by cell phones only, that there were six suspects, including a deputy sheriff, six horses, two trucks and two trailers. The State Police Commander said that he, in his unmarked car and four officers in two official vehicles, were now moving. They should arrive in Nutt in one hour.

Tony barely had time to tell the Sierra County chief to wait another hour before getting started and that the team needed to maintain radio silence at all time, when the next call came in. It was Sunny again.

"Tony, we have a Customs and Borders helo coming in. Ten minutes ago, I sent CBP the picture of the fourth guy with Landing. He's an illegal they hadn't been able to catch before. I'll text you the pilot's number. He'll stay one thousand feet above ground level. That shouldn't interfere with the drones. And the suspects finished their breakfast. They must have scarfed their food! Both trailers turned on 26 at zero-six-four-eight, one minute ago."

That was some good planning! They'll turn onto the county road right around eight. Just like you thought!

Ha! May become a detective when I grow up, Sis.

Will wait. Boys always take longer to mature than women.

~ ~ ~

Waiting was hard for Antonio. He kept wanting to check on progress from everyone.

Patience, Tone. It's happening.

Sunny finally called. "Just got to Nutt. They turned up 57. Going North. All six of them. You're going to tighten that net, Antonio?"

"I'm on it. I'm up the hill just south of Hillsboro. Sierra County is about fifteen minutes behind us. Four deputies. I'm going to send one of their units to wait by the pasture's upper gate. I've advised the Laneys. They are saddling up and are waiting for my call. They will take off from the upper gate. But the cell phone coverage is spotty there at best, so they will look for the helo and the drones. Bill is bringing his drone also, and he is a Ham radio operator. So we'll talk on a simplex frequency and he'll relay to his folks with those little family radios. No one should listen to these. JR is halfway between Hatch and Nutt. We need to give the perps time to get inside the pasture, so we can catch them red-handed. Rick Senior is OK with that."

"Copy that. Good work, Tony!"

~ ~ ~

Chapter 17

A Rustling Party

THE NET WAS TIGHTENING. JR AND HIS OFFICERS were waiting on State Road 57, just south of a little dirt road going nowhere, ending at an old airstream trailer, and running parallel to the southern fence of the Lower Animas pasture. Sunny was not far from where the thieves had gone in. He was flying his drone west, well above the road and the fence. One unit of the Sierra County cops was at the northern entrance to the Lower Animas pasture, the other unit stayed with Tony, still about three miles North of the turn off, hanging on to his every word. Not much happened in their county, but a few drunks and druggies in T or C now and then. Bill was driving his ATV. His knee wasn't doing too bad anymore. He had stopped above the corrals, out of sight in a narrow canyon and was flying his drone. He watched his father and his brother galloping towards him and then slowing their horses about a mile before the corrals. He buzzed them and circled the drone above them, to let them know to wait and not go any further. Then he called Tony to update him on the whereabouts of his family. He also said that he had called his sister and another Livestock inspector so they could join in on the fun. They should arrive in the next hour.

The CBP helicopter still had not shown. That was fine,

thought Antonio. They probably would get seen, although La Migra was a common sight around these parts. The perps had cut the fence and were spreading out on the South side of the pasture. They were using small radios.

JR thought it was time to fly his large drone. He moved his team to the far side of the trailers, so they could not be spotted until the thieves were close by. The bright yellow paint made it easy for everyone to spot the trailers from above as a starting point.

A deputy from Sierra County was an expert radio operator. He soon found their personal frequency. With Tony, they listened to what old man Landing and fat deputy Garcia were saying. They were not moving too fast, walking their horses toward the corrals still about a mile north of the break in the fence, directing the show. Ray and the Mexican were trotting on the West side, according to Bill. The Landing brothers were working the East side. They had already found some cattle and were moving them toward the corrals.

Tony and deputy Johnny Sandoval overheard the Landing boys say: "Hey, these calves look like they were branded about a month ago. Do we still push them?"

The reply came. "Yes, we'll sort them at the corrals. Keep looking for the fresh brands!"

Soon after the other cowboys called in to their bosses. "We got a good bunch. The brand hasn't peeled yet. Should be good to go. We're about a mile west of the corrals. They're gentle and driving good. We can sort them in the corrals in ten-fifteen minutes."

Garcia's old, gruff voice answered. "I'll meet you in the corrals... Brandon, Colter, get your butts over to the corrals with whatever you pick up. Fast! Fresh or older brand, I don't care! We're taking too long already. Something stinks!"

Tony briefed every one in turn about the meeting at the corrals. JR asked for the Laneys' permission to drive straight across the pasture to the corrals. Their answer was: "Go for it. The more, the better. We'll be there soon."

Just about the time everyone was converging to the corrals, the CBP helicopter showed up. Some of the cattle were penned up already. The ones coming in scattered fearfully at the sound of the rotors.

Ray Alvarez and the Mexican kid understood right away that they had been caught. They turned their horses around and galloped to the Northwest, leaving the cattle behind. Above them, the helicopter followed. Rick Junior found them and chased them too.

When they got to the upper gate, one of the Sierra County cops got a hold of their horses. Ray Alvarez gave up and was cuffed, but the Mexican youth ran away from the officers, on foot.

The helicopter pilot put down his bird and ran after the kid, right along side Rick Junior on his horse. The younger Laney threw his rope and caught him by the neck. The pilot cuffed him and handed him to the county cops, saying: "That one's mine. He's CBP property. I'll have a unit pick him up. Don't let him go. We've been looking for that slippery one for over a year! Thanks. Gotta go." He got back in the helicopter

136

and left to help with the other lawmen. Rick Junior galloped back to the others.

Meanwhile at the corrals, Rick Laney Senior had his rifle aimed at the thieves. JR and his four officers cuffed the thieves after getting them off their horses.

Martha Laney and the other inspector got there just as the four thieves were being tossed in the back of the State Police vehicles. She explained that she hadn't realized how the Walking 4 brand could be easily changed to the Double Box, the Landings brand. Same side on the hide. Just a couple of straight lines added with a hot running iron. Cut the ear tags off. And the brands would heal all together.

Ray Alvarez kept claiming his innocence, telling the Sierra County officers and Tony how Garcia had forced him to help, how he was blackmailed by the deputy while he sold dope obtained from across the border. He also told them he had important information that would keep him out of jail, related to a butchered body found in Gila.

Tony wasn't impressed and followed the deputies to the T or C jail.

The Laneys rode and drove home.

JR and his men took the other perps to Deming and impounded their trucks and trailers.

After the CBP helicopter pilot landed at his headquarters, he met with other agents and went to pick up the Mexican cowboy.

Tony got home at six that evening, tired, but elated to have done so well on his first live operation.

You ruled, Tone.
Thanks and did it without you!

~~~

Chapter 18

The Bears' Meeting

CLAIRE SHOWED UP WITH ALMOST FOUR POUNDS of fish, early Saturday afternoon. Bluefin tuna, mackerel and halibut. "That's a lot of fish for just the three of us." She said before she kissed the Tonys.

A minute later, Antonio replied. "Sashimi for us tonight, then ceviche and spicy rolls as appetizers for our party guests tomorrow." Then he started telling her in full details, what he had accomplished the day before.

Antonia cut in the middle of it. "And when he's done, I'll tell you what I did with an Angelman kid and a Two Spirit woman."

Claire was used to their banter and said. "I'm here for two days. I can hear both sides, both stories. Maybe I'll even share one of mine with you. No names. No locations. Just boring stuff, like research and planning. I'm jealous. I rarely get to work operations."

~~~

At the Torres' house, that afternoon, Max and Honaw showed up for their planned meeting. The big ranch house was sprawled in the middle of a large field of mesquite bushes, at the end of a long dirt road.

Young men were playing ball outside. Angel was skipping in the middle of them, laughing. At the sight of strangers, the older boys turned around and protectively helped their younger brother get inside the house.

After everyone had been introduced, Mrs. Torres took Max, Honaw and Angel to a study filled all around with books. An upright piano stood in one corner. Angel took Max by the hand and they moved toward it. They both played some jazzy tune, just made up on the spot.

They kept playing for a few minutes until at once Angel stopped and got off the bench. He took Max by the hand and led him out of the room. His mother looked at him, then left for the kitchen. Angel ambled back to Honaw and squeezed her leg in a fierce embrace. The big bear-woman kneeled by him and returned the hug.

For almost fifteen minutes, silently, they communicated telepathically, the boy standing, quivering slightly, the tall woman still kneeling, holding his hands.

Honaw shared how she feels too much of animals and people's misfortunes and pain around her. How she wished that she could shield herself sometimes from these feelings. She also mentioned that she is not happy the way her tribe is going. They rely too much on the material world, they are getting removed from nature, and are no longer listening to the elders.

Angel squeezed her hands, which made her sigh and then smile.

The boy shared telepathically how he wanted more freedom from his mother, to experience different activities like other children. Although he would not show it, he wanted not to get upset when people laughed at him when he went shopping with his mother. He also wanted to travel, see and feel new things.

It was Honaw's turn to hug Angel, leaving him satisfied, waving his hand in the air with happiness.

When Mrs. Torres returned to the study upon hearing Angel play a few notes on the piano, Honaw talked to her. "Your son wants to experience more in life. He wants to discover new worlds, do some of the things other children his age do, and he wants to do these by himself. He thinks that it's OK to fall down, to hurt himself a little, and to have the shakes, as these will pass on ."

She replied: "Thank you, Mrs. Honaw. I had been thinking of taking him to the children's park in Las Cruces." Turning to the child, she continued. "Would you like to go to the kids' park tomorrow after church, Angel?"

He raised his hands up and shook them.

Honaw then spoke. "You should know that your son has healed a part of myself that was painful to feel. It is easier for me now to accept what I cannot change, to accept the ways of the younger generation, to accept that we are all different. Angel-Osito is a special gift to us all."

~ ~ ~

Chapter 19
Revelry

Claire and the Tonys made sweet love for a good part of the night. The next morning, they woke up radiant, happy to be alive and glad to know each other. They vowed not to wait so long between visits, as much as that could prove possible.

Antonio prepared a delicious breakfast of buckwheat crepes, topped with fresh cream and raspberries. Then he started prepping for the party some of the food he had purchased at the farmers' market, the day before. It had been too long since their friends had been over and they also wanted to show their new acquaintances their appreciation for helping them solve four cases in less than two weeks.

~ ~ ~

Sirena came in early with Mora. They both helped clean up the large backyard. While raking all the sticks and other treasures Tillie had brought into the yard over the tall fence, Mora recounted stories about Angel: his latest antics, his subtle ingenious traits, his gently strumming the school harp after being told how he had helped Max find Honaw. She just had heard from Mrs. Torres how well the meeting between Honaw and Angel had gone. They had agreed to meet more often, as it had been beneficial for both of them.

JR and Bill showed-up at the same time. They set up the tables and chairs.

The mood shifted to one of strong male energy when Sunny arrived. He had Donna, his young, pretty, petite wife, on his arm. He mentioned how sorry he was not to have Antonia present for the party.

As he stated this, JR said aloud: "It's strange I never see one with … Hum! Never mind, just a silly thought."

Sunny must have heard and been on the same wave length when he replied. "Yeah, not possible, I know them too well. I went to school with his sister. Just not possible."

Donna went to the kitchen to see if she could be useful. She and Tony returned to the backyard with bowls and platters filled with colorful foods.

Everyone was gathering around the tables when Lenmana and Max arrived. Tony went to greet them at the front door. "Just in time. We're stating to eat. Welcome. Can I get you a drink? Max, there are some local microbrews in that blue cooler."

Lenmana handed him a large, padded, paper bag. "For the two of you, with my thanks."

Max cut in. "She's been working at it for a week. I helped her with that particular purplish color of the sky. It's one of the hardest to get with natural pigments. Wait till you see it!"

Tony thanked Lenmana, put the gift down and invited them to the tables.

Just then, José and Rosetta showed up. "I smell sweet plantain tostones. What have you fixed us today, Tony?"

Antonio hugged Rosetta. "Eclectic island fare today. From far and not too far. Sicilian antipasto a la Puttanesca, Hawaiian shrimp and cucumber sushi rolls, Japanese spicy hand rolls, mackerel ceviche with sweet potato chips, tostones for the gua-camole and the edamame salsa, Greek mushroom salad, chèvre and figs crostinis, and for my grand finale, your favorite, Rosetta: raspberry-chocolate cashew cheese cake, still in the fridge."

The big woman clapped her hands. "You cooked all day for us. Thank you. Thank you. Now, can we start with desert?"

Everyone cheered and applauded. Next Tony intoned, his voice catching in his throat. "The thanks are to you all. I know Antonia would have liked to be here so we could both thank you for your help. We could not have done it without you. You are all wonderful! I also wish our local Angel could be with us. He was such a help in solving these cases."

Nice speech, boss. Check out your red-haired friend mugging Claire! She can handle him, Sis, but will go rescue her now.

Bill was hovering over Claire, trying to get her full atten-tion. She turned slightly away from him and chimed in with the renewed kudos. Tillie was wrapped up in the euphoria of the moment and ran circles around everyone. Every time around, she would slip right between Bill and Claire, her long wild tail slapping him as she rushed by.

See, she's got you covered. She likes Claire and she is not going to let your cowpoke take her away from us. Go eat. All that nice food makes me hungry!'

As soon as everyone has sat down at the tables, Bill started recounting the aftermath of the catch of the day before. "Tony's plan worked like a charm. Pure clock work. My brother caught this guy that had been stealing from us for the last few years. And James, with Sierra County and the Customs guy caught the wet... the Mexican that they had been looking for. That little pilot dude was fast. I watched him on my drone. He jumped out of his helicopter, the blades were still turning, as he ran down the hill. A few seconds later, with my brother's help, he was bringing back the Mexican in handcuffs..." He took a sip of his beer.

JR took over the story. "At the corrals, we had the three Landings, father and his two sons, and that fat deputy. They tried to tell us that they were looking for some of their cattle that had strayed north. Their ranch is about seventy miles south of the Laneys! They had cut the fence, and were gathering Bill's cattle. The drone caught their voices behind its buzz, and I have them on tape talking about how the brand wasn't too fresh, but fresh enough that they could change it and that in a few months nobody would know the difference."

Sunny could not wait to finish the story. "That pipsqueak Alvarez is already spilling the beans and unloading all kinds of stories about his dad, his neighbors, as well as the Luna County deputy. He thinks that's going to get him off. So, after we got all the perps hand-cuffed and loaded, old man Laney... Sorry Bill." He stopped.

Bill shook his head, smiling. He would probably repeat that story a few more times, as he took over for Sunny. "Old man

Laney, my father, is a tough bird! He said he wished we were still living in the last century. He would have put that bastard out of commission. One less for the gene pool, that's what he likes to say! But he just rode off, his thirty-thirty Winchester back in the scabbard, back to our headquarters."

Tony was curious. "What happens to the trucks, trailers and horses?"

Bill answered. "My sister thinks that my father can buy the two best horses from New Mexico Livestock. The others will go to the Livestock board. But I think we'll have to wait on the equipment. Father thinks either the law will give them to him as payback for what he lost and for trespassing and for the other laws they broke coming onto the ranch. But I think it will probably drag on for a long time, and we'll be lucky to get anything at all."

"At least, you won't be missing calves every time you brand!" Tony added.

"Yes. Thanks Tony. And I'm going to make sure that we tattoo their ears, at least in the Lower Animas. Father had made me the straw boss of that part of the ranch." Bill looked toward Claire for approval, but she was not facing him, but talking softly with Lenmana. Instead, Tony shook his head in approval.

~ ~ ~

After dessert, everyone was silent for a bit.

Chuckling, Rosetta said. "Too much food slows down the brain! But that cake was the best! Don't write me the recipe, just make me one like that, once a month. But only once a month. My waistline is already bursting the seams of my panties." Everyone joined in the laughter.

Later, she went to sit by JR and bending over toward him, whispered. "Have your met Lenmana?"

"Yes! The Native American woman. She seems very nice. It's hard to tell she is blind. Is she totally blind or can she see a little? Do you know?" JR whispered back.

"She is totally blind. Antonia told me that she had some vision until puberty. Then everything went dark. She is an amazing weaver."

JR was staring at Lenmana. Then he turned back to Rosetta. "What amazes me is that all the Natives have such poor eyesight. It must be genetic."

Rosetta frowned, shook her head a couple of times and looked impatiently at him. "You still don't know what is wrong with your rookies' training. Do you?" It was hard for her to keep her voice down, she was so upset with the big policeman.

JR took both her hands in his, then whispered. "You're right. You're absolutely right. I've been training my officers to believe in generalities, in establishing prejudice with the various kind of people we deal with, before we can make an impartial judgement. When Tony told me about the missing Native, I immediately flashed on a drunken Indian. Now I know that I was wrong. That is the way I was trained, but that is not an excuse. In the future I will be careful to train my officers and the trainers who will replace me next year, without any built-in prejudices. Thank you, Rosetta."

"Good! Now, can I tell you about Two Spirit people?" She asked him with a grin.

~~~

Antonio and Sirena brought back empty dishes and glassware to the kitchen. Tony remembered the package Lenmana had given him earlier and took it to the backyard.

He sat down and carefully pulling the strings of the bow made of twisted strands of purple wool, he opened the package sitting on his lap. A weaving.

Feels like wool. Soft colors from natural dyes, no doubt.

Tony gently unwrapped the tapestry, stretching it horizontally, like a runner, with a story for all to see.

A blue dog and a green cat inside a cream-colored circle. Tamed bears and lions! She knows too much.

A couple of friends came over to have a closer look.

On top a bluish-purple sky laced with stylized brown lightning bolts. Is Rosetta involved in this? And below, a light green river. Déjà vu, brother.

After listening to much praises about the weaving, Antonio went to sit by the blind woman.

"Lenmana, I did not expect anything like this. You have already paid us... This is magnificent! Thank you. My sister and I really appreciate this work of art."

With a very slight bow, she replied. "I did not expect that you would know and understand the spiritual world we live in. This is one of the reflections of who you may be."

It certainly reflects us! Dog and cat. Fire and water. Bluish and green. Different but the same. Peace and love, brother.

Antonia was sending him the internal message, as Lenmana was saying: "I hope it reflects both your inner states, and that you find peace now that you two are getting along again."

Another one who found us out, Sis!

~ ~ ~

Max guided Lenmana to the bench where sat Sirena, then left to go inside the house as soon as she was seated.

With a serious face and to the point, she asked. "Ms. Sirena, would you be interested in someone teaching weaving at the school?"

Smiling, Sirena replied. "And who would that someone be? What would she need? What would she achieve?"

"I would need a classroom for a two-hour classes once a week. It cannot be a mandatory class and only people who want to attend can participate. I would need the cost of the fuel refunded or my transport to and from home provided. It would start after I come back to the valley in a couple of months. I would need wood, wool and other materials for building and working the looms. In turn, I will teach, only to those who are willing to learn the elders' ways, how to build a loom and how to weave in the traditional Diné way."

Sirena continued: "What else do you need? I can pay a small stipend for your time and effort."

In her shy, slow tone, Lenmana replied. "I would like for Mother Honaw, Max and myself as well, to be able to spend some time, even a short time with Master Angel, if agreeable with his mother. And I almost forgot, Max has a package for Master Angel."

Sirena stood up, and faced the Native woman. "May I hug you?"

She embraced Lenmana and said: "Welcome to our family."

Max handed Sirena a brown, unsealed, paper bag. "Thank you. Can I open it? I am supposed to inspect anything prior to handing it to Angel."

She pulled out a soft brown leather pouch, hand-stitched with thin, yellow, leather strips.

"Oh! Max. A sling-bag for his computer! It looks like it's the right size. I bet he'll be using it all the time. You made this, yes? So you will have to come see him using it, sometime soon. One person at a time is best."

Sirena got up and hugged Max, disappearing inside his big bear arms.

~ ~ ~

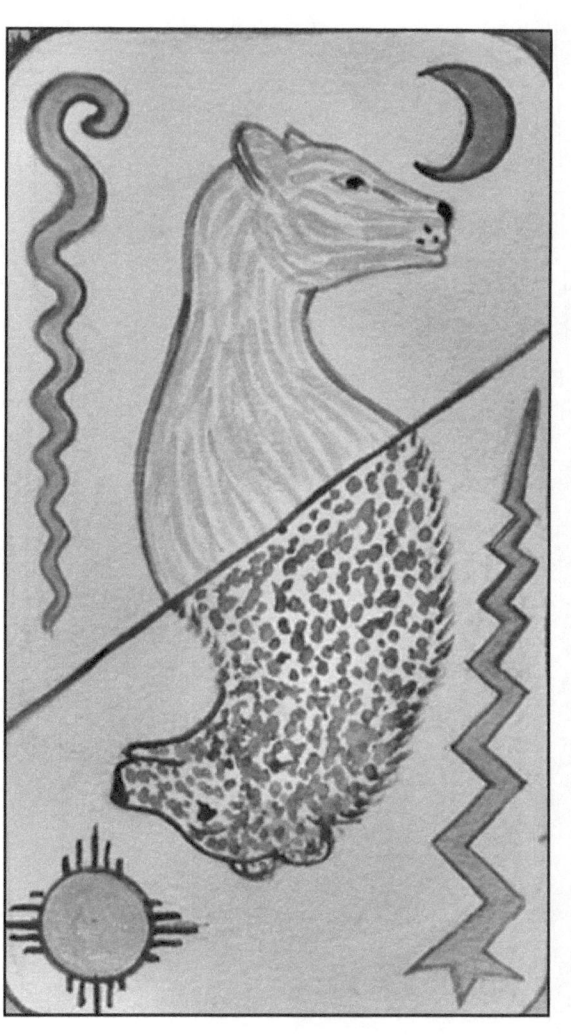